BARE KNUCKLE BITCH

ISBN   978-1481804554

Also available:

The Meat Wagon
Skinhead Away
The Fall of Humpty Dumpty
Punk Rock Nursing Home

1

So I'm in the local night club with my mate Shaz, yeah? The Zone, it says on the big neon sign above the door, but most people call it The Meat Market. It's the sort of place you go to if you want to find random people to fuck without having to worry about any of that soppy romance bollocks. I'm sure you know the sort of place I mean; you've probably been to one yourself a few times, right? Low lights so you can't see how ugly everyone is, loud music so you can't hear how fucking boring they are. The perfect pick-up joint for freaks of all ages, yeah?

Anyway, we're checking out the studs lined up along the bar, trying to decide which ones are worth bothering with. Most of them are fat bastards in their thirties with huge beer guts flopping down over their belts like an old woman's tits, so there's not much to choose from. There is one reasonable looking guy at the end of the bar though. Not that he would win any beauty contests, mind. He's dog fucking rough in the face department, and his clothes look like he's slept in them for a month, but he does have this massive bulge sticking out of the front of his trousers that catches my eye.

"See anything you fancy?" Shaz yells in my ear.

Shaz is the same age as me, but she looks a few years older. We grew up on the same council estate and went to the same shitty schools together, so we've known each other pretty much forever. My dad calls her a trollop and says she's a bad influence on me, but he doesn't know the half of it.

"That one's quite cute," I shout back, nodding my head toward bulge-guy. It's like he can hear me over the loud thumping music or something, because he looks straight at me and winks.

Shaz shakes her head and sighs. "Fucking hell Abby,

3

try looking beyond his cock. He's fucking skint, you can tell that a mile off. You'd be lucky to get a drink out of him, never mind anything else."

"Well what about that one then?" I point at one of the fatties, choosing him at random.

"Are you kidding? Look at his shoes. Fucking Hush Puppies? Get real, Abby."

"Well which one would you go for?"

Shaz smiles, and points her finger at one of the other fatties. "Armani suit, not cheap in that size. You need to get them made especially, you can't just pick one up off the fat cunt rail in Tesco. See those shoes? Paul Smith brogues, three hundred quid a pop. And look at the way he's standing, you can tell he's used to ordering people around. Probably middle management at least, but more likely some sort of fucking company director. Either way he's fucking loaded."

"Right," I say. I'll have to take her word for it, I know fuck all about men's clothes and the way this one's standing doesn't look any different to the way all the other fat bastards are standing. "So who's having him then, you or me?"

"You can have him, I'll pick one of the others."

"Right, okay. See you later then, yeah?"

I walk up to the bar and squeeze myself in next to the one Shaz pointed out for me. The barman looks at me and nods, asking if I need serving. I shake my head and he walks away to serve someone else. The fatty on my left looks in my direction and smiles, thinking he's in with a chance. I scowl at him and he looks away sharply. His face turns the colour of a slapped arse.

I turn my head to look at the over-stuffed Armani suit on my right. He stares straight ahead at the optics behind the bar but it's obvious he knows I'm here from the way his hand shakes when he picks up his drink. Great, he's one of those fucking shy bastards. That means I'll have to make all the moves instead of just standing here looking pretty. I nudge him with my elbow and watch the rolls of fat ripple for a few seconds until they settle down again.

"Hi," I yell when he doesn't look in my direction. No reply. I can see sweat breaking out on his forehead. Fucking hell, he's not going to make this easy for me, is he? I stroke the back of his hand with my fingertips. He jumps as if I've just fucking scratched him or something, and turns toward me.

"Hi," I yell again. I flash him my warmest smile and hope he doesn't make a run for it. If he does I'll have to go back to Shaz and start the selection process all over again.

"Um... hello. Do you come here often?" he says.

I laugh. Well at least he can fucking talk, even if what he does say is corny as fuck. "Yeah, I come here all the time. You going to buy me a drink then or what?"

"Um... sure, what'll you have?"

"A pint of Guinness and a whisky chaser."

He pulls out a brown leather wallet and I can't help noticing how stuffed full of money it is when he plucks out a tenner and waves it at the barman. There must be a few hundred quid in there, easy. I turn and give Shaz a double thumbs up while he's distracted with the barman. She smiles back at me in that smug bastard way people do when they know they've been proven right.

He buys my drinks and I down half the Guinness in one go, then wipe the froth from my mouth with the back of my hand.

"So, um, what do you do for a living?" he asks. As if he gives a fuck what I do or who I do it with. But I might as well humour him, it's only polite.

"I work the till in a burger joint. How about you?"

"I'm a stockbroker." He says this as if I'm supposed to be impressed, but I'll be fucked if I know what one of those is. Probably something to do with warehouses, or making sure a supermarket's shelves don't run empty.

"Oh yeah?" I shout. "That's nice."

"My name's Alan."

I shrug and pick up my Guinness, drain the rest of it. The whisky follows it down, and I get a warm glow spreading down my throat and into my chest.

"So what's yours?" he yells.

"I'll have another pint of Guinness, Alan."

"No, I mean, um, what's your name?"

"Abby."

"Pleased to meet you, Abby."

He holds out his hand. I look at it. Who the fuck wants to shake hands when they're picking up some random woman at a bar? He holds it there a few more seconds, then takes the hint and reaches for his wallet. He orders himself an alcohol-free beer, obviously worried whether he'll be able to perform or not when the time comes.

The fat cunt on my left peels himself away from the bar and waddles off to the toilets like a hippo that's just learnt how to walk on two legs, so I put a bit of space between me and my new friend Alan. He's sweating like a pig, but it's not the nice, heady aroma of a proper man. It's the sort of greasy chips and curry stench you always get from fat blokes. I lean back against the bar and take another long drink.

"So, um, you fancy going somewhere a bit quieter, Abby?" Alan asks my tits.

I answer on their behalf. "Nah, I like it in here. Besides, I'm barred from most of the pubs in town."

"I, um, wasn't really thinking of another pub."

Here it comes. Two measly fucking drinks I've had from the cunt and he already thinks he's fully paid up. What the fuck is it with men these days? I'd need at least ten pints before I even considered having that lard-arse pounding on top of me. I'd need the anaesthetic for when he crushes my fucking ribs.

"Maybe later," I yell. "The night's still young and all that." I drain the rest of my pint and hand the glass to Alan. "Your round, yeah?"

While he gets the drinks in I look to see what Shaz is doing. The bulge-guy is sitting with her, yelling something into her ear. Shaz is laughing. I frown. All that bollocks she came out with about him being skint, and all along she just wanted him for herself.

"Is something wrong, Abby?" Alan must've picked up on my annoyance with Shaz, so I smile to reassure him everything's fine.

"Nothing at all, Alan." I raise my pint glass toward him. "Cheers." He picks up his alcohol-free beer and chinks my glass, smiles back.

I look back at Shaz, try to catch her eye to show her how fucking pissed off I am, but she's too busy throwing herself at bulge-guy. His arm is round her shoulder, and her hand is resting on his thigh, brushing the tip of his bulge with her thumb. He leans in for a kiss and gropes her tits. I hope it's just a fucking rolled up sock he's got stuffed down his pants, it'd serve Shaz right for lining me up with this fat sweaty bastard and keeping the best guy in the whole fucking place for herself.

I turn back to the bar and try to think of something to say to Alan. I mean, what do you say to someone you have absolutely nothing whatsoever in common with, and who makes your fucking skin crawl just thinking about him? I can't think of anything, so I just ask the obvious question.

"So, Alan, have you got any rubber johnnies on you?"

Fuck it, straight to the point, that's me. Well it certainly gets Alan's attention anyway. He stares at me with his mouth open as if he can't believe what I've just said. His face flushes red, his hands start to tremble. He fiddles with the knot of his tie.

"Um, no. But I could, um, get some from the machine in the toilets?"

I smile and wink at him, and a huge soppy grin spreads over his face. Like a little kid on Christmas day who's woke up to a room full of presents, or a twelve year old boy who's just lost his virginity.

"Yeah, you do that. And make sure they're ribbed, yeah? Oh, and get those strawberry flavoured ones too if you can. I don't like the taste of rubber."

I never thought it was possible for a face to go as red as his. I wouldn't be surprised if his head just fucking exploded right there in front of me.

"Oh. Um, yes, I– of course I will."

I smile to myself as he scoots off to the toilets to buy the johnnies. I lean back on the bar to watch, and shake my head at the comical way he walks. I look for Shaz to give her an update, but she's not there. And neither is bulge-guy. Great, just my fucking luck.

Alan strides back. He pats his breast pocket and grins like a fucking loon. "I got them, Abby," he says. "Where do you want to do it?"

"Hold your horses, lover. How about another drink first?"

My head's starting to get comfortably mashed from the Guinness, but a few more won't hurt. I wonder if Shaz is having a good time with bulge-guy, whether he's one of those fumble and shoot types or if he's one of those fucking marathon-men who last for hours. I hope it's the former.

Alan gulps down his alcohol-free beer. I take my time and sip my Guinness, all the while keeping an eye out for Shaz. She's taking her fucking time, she's had long enough now to bang the entire fucking night club never mind just one bloke. Lucky cow.

I've still got half a pint left when Alan starts talking to my tits again, telling them it's time to go somewhere quiet. Fuck it, might as well make my move. Shaz can't be much longer, surely.

"Hundred quid," I say. The look of pure innocent shock on his face is fucking priceless. I wish I had my phone ready so I could take a photo, but it's too late now.

"Um... sorry?" he says. He looks at me wide-eyed.

"Hundred quid. In advance, yeah?"

"But I bought you all those drinks," he splutters.

"Yeah, and?"

"Um... okay. Just so that we're clear, what does a hundred pounds buy me?"

I shrug, playing it cool. I'd been expecting him to haggle, or maybe even just tell me to fuck off when he found out it wasn't going to be free. But the glint in his eye tells me he's definitely interested. I give him a coy smile. "Whatever you want it to buy you, Alan."

I can practically hear those cogs in his head grinding against each other. He grins and reaches for his wallet, peels off five twenty pound notes and thrusts them into my hand. I pull out my low-cut top and stuff the money inside my bra for safe keeping. Alan leans forward to get himself a good look at his investment.

"Wait there, I need to go to the toilet," I tell him. "This Guinness has gone straight through me."

He's obviously not as daft as he looks, because he follows me to the ladies. "I'll wait for you here," he says when I push open the pink door. "Don't be long, will you?" I can feel his eyes burning into my arse as I let go of the door and it swings shut on him.

Both the cubicles are full, and I have to stand there with my legs crossed so I don't piss myself while I wait. It takes fucking ages, but eventually I hear a bolt slide open on one of the cubicle doors. Some middle-aged tart with smudged makeup staggers out and heads toward the mirror.

I'm in the cubicle like a fucking shot. I hitch up my miniskirt and pull down my knickers before I've even got the door shut. I don't bother locking it, there isn't enough time. I squat down on the toilet and sigh in relief while the piss gushes out of me.

I look for some toilet paper to wipe myself with, but the bog-roll dispenser is empty, just a cardboard tube to taunt me with. Fucking great. I bounce up and down on the toilet seat to shake off as may drops as I can, then use the palm of my hand for the rest. I pull up my knickers and open the cubicle door. I go to the sink and turn the tap on, rinse my hands under the cold water.

The old tart is still here, standing in front of the mirror trying to repair her makeup. But she's so fucking pissed she just makes it look even worse than it did before. She looks like something from a fucking horror movie, and I pity whichever poor sap has to bang that monster tonight. With a final pout at the mirror, she staggers past me toward the exit. Alan holds the door open while she walks through it. After she's gone he stares in at me.

"Are you going to be much longer, Abby?"

I look at my reflection in the mirror and sigh. "Another five minutes and I'll be all yours, yeah?"

I splash cold water onto my face and hear the door thump shut. I spin round, expecting to see Alan with his pants round his ankles waddling toward me with his cock out, but I'm all alone in here. I rub the water off my face and shake my hands over the sink. There's no paper towels, and the electric dryer has an *Out of Order* sign on it, so I'll need to drip-dry.

I go back into the cubicle and lock the door behind me. I put the toilet lid down and sit on it, then take out my phone. I unlock it and prod Shaz's picture in my contacts, put the phone to my ear.

It rings out to voicemail.

I shake my head, hang up, and try again. This time she answers, out of breath. I can hear loud, rhythmic grunting sounds in the background.

"Where the fuck are you, Shaz?"

"I'm– ah! Harder! I'm a bit– ah! Busy at the moment Abby, can you call back later?"

"Are you *fucking* someone?"

"No. Ah! I mean yes, faster! That's it, you fucking bastard."

"For fuck's sake Shaz, I'm ready to go with that fat bastard and I need you to watch my back. Where the fuck are you, anyway?"

"Ah! Ah! Hold on Abby, I won't be long. I'll come and find you when I'm done."

"Yeah well tell your fucking stud to hurry up, I can't wait forever."

I look at my phone as it grunts and squeals at me. I hear a slapping sound and Shaz cries out. Her stud moans, shooting his load, and I put the phone back to my ear.

"Shaz? Have you finished?"

It's a while before she answers, and she's still out of breath. "I'm on my way Abby, where are you now?"

"I'm in the women's toilets. You need to get here now, I don't think he'll wait much longer."

"I'm only next door in the gents, I'll make my way outside now and wait for you there."

In the gents? Fucking hell, you wouldn't catch me doing it in there. Those cunts are just fucking animals the way they piss all over the floor.

"Right," I say. "Let me know when you're outside, yeah?"

"Will do, Abby. See you, Steve." I hear a man's voice mumble something, then the sound of someone pissing into water fades into the background. "Just on my way out the door now, no sign of your friend though. Maybe he changed his mind?"

I end the call and open the cubicle door. Alan stares in at me. He takes me by surprise, but it doesn't take me long to compose myself.

"Sorry I took so long," I say. I smile and loop my arm through his.

"That's okay Abby, you're here now."

I lead him out of the night club and steer him toward the back alley that runs behind it. Shaz watches us from across the road. Her face looks flushed under the orange glow of the streetlamp she leans against.

Alan stops abruptly. "I have a car just down the road, it's got a really comfortable back seat."

Shit, think fast. No way am I getting in a fucking car with him, he could be some sort of fucking psycho for all I know.

I spin around and stick my tongue down his throat to give myself a bit more thinking time. Fuck me, when was the last time he brushed his teeth? His mouth tastes fucking rank, like he's been eating dog shit or something.

"I like it rough, and I want you to fuck me down here," I say, pointing toward the alley. "Away from the cameras, yeah?"

"Ah, okay. Good thinking."

He follows me eagerly now, and when I reach the alleyway I glance over at Shaz to make sure she's still there. She gives me a thumbs-up in reply. I take Alan a few yards into the alley and find a good spot behind a large industrial-size dumpster and pull him toward it.

He pins me against the wall and gropes my tits while his mouth goes to work on my neck. It feels like a slug crawling across me, and I shudder in revulsion. Alan takes that as a sign I'm ready for action, and pulls down his

12

trousers. He hitches up my miniskirt and smears cock-snot all over my thighs while he yanks at the elastic on my knickers. I snap my legs together and push him away with both hands.

"Put a johnny on, yeah?"

He blinks at me for a few seconds and nods. He pulls one out of his breast pocket and bites the seal open, spits out a sliver of silver foil. He plucks the rubber out and grins when he shows me it. It's bright fucking red and there's a smiley face on the end of it with the little spunk-bubble forming the nose. It looks like something a fucking clown would wear to an orgy, and I can't help wondering if it will squeak if I squeeze it hard enough. He sticks it over the end of his cock and rolls it down with his thumb and forefinger.

Shaz creeps up behind him like a pantomime villain, up on her toes with her arms outstretched at the sides for balance.

"Is that you Abby?" she says quietly.

Alan jumps and spins around in shock. Shaz's eyes drop down to the bright red rubber-coated cock smiling at her, and her eyes widen in disbelief. Alan pulls his trousers up and spins back to me. His face turns the same shade of red as the cock poking out of his fly.

"All right Shaz," I say, unable to keep the grin off my face. I love this part.

"Is this pervert bothering you?" she says with a straight face. I don't know how she does it. Practice, I suppose, but I know I wouldn't be able to manage it without sniggering. She must be in a good mood about something if she wants to play this line instead of just kicking the fuck out of him and taking his wallet. It's been a while since we've used it, and I'm probably getting a bit too old for it now, but I might as well play along.

"No, he's my fella."

Alan turns to Shaz and nods his head vigorously. Shaz looks him up and down with a sneer. Her gaze lingers on his cock. "You do know she's only fourteen?"

Alan looks at me and his mouth gapes open. "Um... god, no, I didn't. Are you sure?"

"Hey baby," I say. I reach out for his cock and give it a gentle squeeze. "What difference does my age make? I've still got all the right parts, and they're all in full working order."

Alan looks at me as if I'm some sort of fucking monster, and his cock shrivels up. He stuffs it into his trousers and zips up, then backs away from me with his hands held out to ward me off. I bet if he had a fucking crucifix he'd be holding that up too. *Get thee behind me foul wench of Satan*, or some bollocks like that.

"Look, I'm, ah... I think I should just go," he says.

"Not so fast, Romeo," Shaz says, heading him off. She takes out her phone and makes sure he sees it. "I should really report this to the police."

"No, no," he says quickly. "There's no need for that, I'll be on my way."

"We can't have fucking pedos walking the streets and raping little kids, it's not right." She thumbs the digit nine on her phone.

Alan looks like he's about to shit himself. "No, please, my wife will kill me," he whines. He reaches for his wallet and pulls it out. "Look, I'll pay you anything you want, just don't call the police okay?"

Shaz's thumb hovers over the phone, ready to dial the next number. "I don't know about that, it's my public duty to report a crime when I see one taking place."

Alan pulls notes from his wallet and holds them out to Shaz at arm's length. His hands are shaking so much I can't even see what denomination they are, but there's a fucking lot of them. Shaz hesitates, and then sighs. A bit theatrically if you ask me, but Alan is too relieved when she takes the money to notice.

"Thank you," he says, and turns to leave.

I don't know if you've ever seen a really fat man run, but it's pretty comical to watch and I can't help laughing as he shambles away with his arms flailing.

Shaz waits until he's out of sight before she shares out the takings. I don't tell her about the hundred quid I've got stuffed inside my bra, I deserve a bit extra for all the worry she put me through when she left me on my own. All in all, my share comes to a hundred and ninety quid, not bad for a couple of hours work. That's a lot better than what I make working at the burger joint for a whole fucking week.

"So what do you want to do now?" Shaz asks. "Back in The Meat Market and get tanked up?"

I shake my head. I've already had enough booze, all I want now is a bag of chips to soak it up and then fuck off home to bed. "Nah, I've got work in the morning. I need to get some kip or I'll be like a fucking zombie all day."

"You fucking lightweight," Shaz says with a sneer. "Go on, one more drink won't hurt."

I sigh. Fuck it, she's right. Just one drink though, and that's my lot. After that it's straight home to bed.

"Go on then," I say. "So what was that guy like that you were fucking? Was his bulge genuine, or was it just for show?"

Shaz smiles and taps on her phone. "God, yeah. I've got a photo of it here, see for yourself."

She tilts the phone toward me. I look at the screen and frown. Great, just my fucking luck.

2

I can't be arsed going to work. My head's banging and I feel like fucking shit. My throat's as dry as a granny's cunt and my stomach feels like I've done ten rounds with Mike fucking Tyson. There must've been something wrong with that bag of chips I ate last night, because it obviously hasn't agreed with me. Maybe I should grass the chip shop up and see if I can claim some compensation, I'll look into that later. Meanwhile I'll get my mum to phone in sick for me and go back to sleep. I'll go in tomorrow if I'm feeling any better by then. If not, fuck it. Yeah, that's what I'll do. In a minute or so. I'll just rest here a bit longer first.

The next thing I know the BBC News music blares up through the floorboards. Fucking parents, they've got no consideration for invalids like me. I think about yelling at them to turn the fucker down, but I'm already wide awake so I might as well get up now.

I swing out of bed and put my bunny slippers on, then pad across the landing to the bathroom in my nightie. I put my mouth to the cold water tap and turn it on, gasp when the cold water hits me. I drink my fill and splash some on my face, then rub it off with the grimy towel hanging over the side of the bath. I try not to think about where else the towel's been since it last got washed, some things you're better off not knowing.

After a quick shit I wash my hands, put my tracksuit on, and go downstairs. The news is in full swing by now, something about terrorists in Libya or wherever. You know, boring crap like that. Dad's watching it, riveted to the TV set as if it's something fucking important. "You need to keep up with current affairs," he always says when I ask if I can change the channel. Fuck knows why he wants to know what's going on in the world, though. He never leaves the fucking house, he just sits there all day while my mum goes out to work and then expects her to clean up after him when she gets back.

He's a bit of a cunt too, always has been. My earliest childhood memories are of my dad shouting and screaming all the time. He never hit me, in fact he never really had much to do with me at all while I was growing up, but I learnt to hate him from a very young age. It wasn't until I started school that I found out all dads weren't like that. I guess I was just unlucky. Story of my life, yeah?

"Good afternoon, Abigail," dad says. "So what time did you roll in last night? Or was it this morning?"

"Dunno," I say. Which is true. Mum and dad were snoring away when I got home, and mum must've unplugged my clock to use the hoover while I was out because it was just flashing 12:00 at me and I couldn't be arsed setting it from my phone.

"You're not at work today, then."

"Well duh," I say, and flop down on the settee. Clouds of dust fly up and make me sneeze.

"Day off or are you just twagging it?"

I shrug. "What difference does it make?"

"Yeah well, you'd best not lose that job. There's the rent to pay, remember. We can't afford to keep you for free, you know. We're not a charity."

Can't afford not to sponge off me, he means. You'd think he'd be proud of me getting a job, it's not like there's many of them to go around, and I don't think he's ever worked in his entire life. It might be just minimum wage but it's a fuck sight better than the alternative. But no, all dad cares about is the handouts he gets off me every pay day. "To pay for your board and keep," he says, then sends my mum off to the shops with it for a crate of beer.

"Are you listening to me?" dad yells.

"Yeah, yeah."

17

Like fuck I am. It's always the same bollocks from him. Fat waste of space that he is. Fuck knows why mum puts up with him the way she does, I know I wouldn't if I had the choice. One day I'll get together a deposit for a bedsit, then I'll be straight out of the fucking door. Let's see where he gets his beer money from then.

Dad's still nagging away when the weather forecast comes on, but I've had enough so I get my boots from the hallway and put them on.

"And where do you think you're going?" he demands to know.

"Out," I say.

"Where to?"

"Don't know yet, just out."

"What about my dinner?"

"What about it?"

"I haven't had nothing all day and your mum forgot to make me something before she went out to work."

"Can't you just make a sandwich or something?"

Dad shakes his head. "There's no bread left. Can you get me some from the shops?"

"Go on then," I sigh. Anything for a quiet life.

"And a packet of fags from Mike down the road. Oh, and a bag of chips to go with the bread."

"Anything else?" A stupid fucking question I know, and I regret asking it the minute it rolls off my tongue.

"A couple of cans of Special Brew from the offy would go down a treat."

"And I suppose you want me to pay for it all?"

"You're a good 'un, lass."

Yeah, right. When I'm splashing the cash. Any other time he's always moaning about what a fucking disgrace I am. The lazy cunt's never done a day's work in his entire life, but *I'm* the fucking disgrace? Yeah, whatever.

Well I get him his stuff, because I'm soft like that. I go

18

round to Mike's house for the knockoff ciggies, then down the chippy, then call in at the beer-off on the way back for the booze and bread. The ungrateful bastard doesn't even say thanks when I hand them to him, just shuffles off into the kitchen with a grunt. I don't know why I fucking bother.

The cunt's got me all worked up now, so I need to let off a bit of steam. I leave the front door open, hoping some mad axeman will take the hint and do my dad in, and make my way to the gym. It's a bit of a fucking dump, just your average back street dive, yeah? All peeling paint and graffiti on the outside, a stink of blood and sweat on the inside. Just my kind of place.

I push through the door and nod toward Big Al, the owner. He grunts at me and turns his attention back to the two lads sparring in the ring. They've got those stupid padded helmets on and they're just standing there taking turns to hit each other, like they're fucking robots bolted down to the canvas or something. No real flair for the sport, you see. Unlike me. I reckon I could take them both on at once, no fucking bother.

I head into the changing room at the back of the gym. I open up a locker and strip down to my sports bra and pants. I stuff my street clothes into the locker and pull out a vest and shorts. I slip them on, then bang the locker door shut and turn the key.

When I turn around Big Al's standing in the doorway, watching me. Fuck knows how long he's been there, but if he wants to perv over me I couldn't care less. That's probably the only thrill he ever gets these days, since his wife died, so I don't begrudge him it. As long as he sticks to just looking, anyway. If he ever touches me I'll break his fucking arms and legs. I frown at him as I brush past, just to drive the point home, and his face goes red.

I go straight to one of the punch-bags and smack the fuck out of it, imagining it's my dad that I'm whacking.

Dad lurches back with each blow, then swings toward me on his chain. I dodge out of his way and punch him in the face again.

"You up for a bit of sparring, Abby? Show these lads what you're supposed to do?"

I hit the leather bag one more time and turn toward Big Al. He holds up a pair of boxing gloves. I look at the two lads playing patty-cake in the ring and smile.

"Yeah, can do."

I take the boxing gloves and put them on, turn back to the punch-bag to try them out for size.

"Go easy on them Abby, it's their first time," Big Al says.

"Yeah, no worries," I say, walking up to the ring.

"Aren't you going to put a helmet on?"

I turn back to Big Al and smile. "Yeah, like I'm going to need one of those."

"Okay listen up, lads," Big Al says. He thumps the palm of his hand down on the boxing ring's canvas to get their attention. "Abby here is going to show you how it's done."

The two lads stop what they're doing and look at me. One smirks to himself. I step through the ropes into the ring and take up my boxing stance. Gloves up, skipping from one foot to the other, I glide toward the centre of the ring and show them a few moves by punching the air just short of their faces. They look at each other, suitably impressed, and one raises his gloves in front of his face. I dart in underneath them and punch him in the stomach. He folds over, groaning. I dance back, looking at his mate. He stands there with his arms by his sides and stares at me wide-eyed.

"Go on son, she won't bite," Big Al says.

But the lad doesn't look too convinced about that. He backs away toward the ropes, shaking his head. It's the other one that comes for me, his eyes blazing. He takes a swing and I duck beneath it. He stumbles forward when his fist hits nothing but thin air, and I dart around behind him. In a street fight I'd whack him on the back of the neck and send him sprawling, but in the ring it's different rules. I hop from one foot to the other and wait for him to turn to face me again.

He lurches forward, takes another swing. I block it with my left and jab with the right. His padded helmet takes most of the impact, but I can tell from the look on his face that I hurt him. He steps back, gloves raised. I dance toward him and feign another blow to the stomach. The gloves drop, his upper body leans forward, and I take advantage of the opening he's given me to get a few quick jabs into his face before he realises his mistake.

"Okay, that's enough Abby," Big Al says just as I'm starting to enjoy myself. "Now listen up, lads. Did you see the way she kept moving the whole time? That's what I want to see you doing. And use your gloves for defence, not just attack. Thanks Abby," he adds when I climb out of the ring and hand him the boxing gloves.

There's someone watching me with a dopey-looking smile on his face. He's about the same age as me, maybe a few years older, but his clothes look like something out of a fucking 1980s documentary about skinhead street fashion. Bleached denim jeans with red braces hanging down the sides, massive fuck-off boots that go half way up his legs, and a white T-shirt with the words Argy Bargy printed on it. He's got short-cropped hair, and a blue borstal spot tattooed on his cheek. There's some proper tattoos on his arms, naked women and bulldogs, that kind of thing, and a spidery home-made one on his neck that's probably supposed to be barbed wire but just looks like a scribble.

I can feel his eyes follow me across the gym as I return to the punch-bag. I'm not angry any more, I've already worked that out of my system, so I just slap it around half-heartedly for something to do.

"Cool moves for a chick."

I spin around to pummel the cheeky bastard and he backs away with his hands raised, that same dopey smile still on his face.

"You ever think of doing it professionally?" he asks.

Well that's the lamest fucking pick-up line I've ever heard, and I can't help smiling at how bad it is. But he must think I'm smiling at him, the daft cunt, and he holds out his fist for me to bump. Predictably enough, it's got HATE tattooed on the knuckles in shaky blue ink.

"I'm Dave," he says.

I shrug and look him up and down. "Yeah, so?" Like I give a fuck what he calls himself.

"Aren't you going to tell me your name?"

I turn back to the punch-bag and start smacking it around again. "What's it to you?" I say between grunts.

"I could make you some serious money."

I stop punching the bag and turn back to face him. I mean, come on, who the fuck can ever resist those magic words? I've been skint my whole fucking life, yeah? I grew up with fuck all, and now I'm working my dad pinches half my wages so I can't even afford a decent piss up more than once a week. Not without the little extras I make with Shaz at The Meat Market, anyway. The idea of making some serious money, even some fucking silly money, is very enticing.

"Doing what?" I say, suddenly suspicious.

"Doing what you do best."

I scowl at him. "Fuck off, I'm no prossie. And even if I was I wouldn't work for no fucking pimp."

"No, no," he says quickly, palms facing me. "I mean fighting."

"What, like amateur boxing you mean? I looked into

22

that once but it pays fuck all unless you turn pro."

He laughs. "No, I mean fighting. I know a guy who pays three hundred quid per fight, win or lose."

I look at him for any hint that this is just some sort of fucking wind up, but I can't see any. I mean, three hundred quid? That's a lot of fucking money, I could get a deposit on a bedsit for that much. But it all sounds too good to be true.

"What sort of fight would pay that much?"

He grins. "Not here. Meet me at the café on the corner of James Street in an hour if you're interested."

I shrug. "Yeah, okay."

"Laters then," he says, walking away. As he reaches the door he calls out over his shoulder, "So what's your name then?"

I ignore him and go back to punching the bag. I'll listen to what he's got to say, but if he turns out to be full of shit I'll kick his fucking head in for wasting my time.

* * *

The skinhead's already at the greasy spoon when I get there, scoffing down a plate of egg and chips. He looks up and waves at me like an excited kid who's just seen the fucking queen or something, and I make my way to his table. I slide into the bucket seat opposite and snatch a chip from his plate.

"Oi, that's me dinner," he whines, but he doesn't make any attempt to stop me pinching another.

A waitress comes over in an apron covered in stains from fuck knows what and I order a cheese and tomato sandwich and a mug of strong tea. I sit back and look at Dave while I wait. His table manners are worse than my dad's. He slides his fork under the fried egg and lifts it up to his mouth, but it falls off halfway there and splats down onto the table. There's runny yolk all over the table when he picks it up with his fingers and puts it back on his plate. He picks up a chip and rubs it around in the yolk on the table.

My sandwich arrives wrapped in clingfilm, and I tear it open. I lift off the top half of the bap to have a look, there's about twenty strands of grated cheese inside, and one measly slice of soggy tomato. There's probably more margarine smeared on the side of the cracked mug she plonks down beside me than there is on the sandwich, but at least the tea looks strong enough.

"You gonna eat that or just stare at it all day?" Dave asks.

I put the lid back on the sandwich and take a bite. The soggy tomato comes out whole and flops down my chin, hanging from my teeth. I pull it out of my mouth and put it back inside the sandwich where it belongs, and wipe the seeds off my chin with the back of my hand. Dave smirks, but he's got no need to talk with egg yolk all over his face. But I guess we do make a good pair of slobs between us, so I can't help smiling.

"So what's this about fights then?" I ask after I've swallowed down the cheese and bread.

Dave leans forward. "Mate of mine organises them," he says. "He's always looking for new talent. You interested?"

"What kind of fights are they?"

He shrugs. "The unregulated kind. You know, the ones that don't exactly get advertised anywhere?"

I don't know what he's going on about, for all I know he's just making it all up to get in my knickers, but I decide to play along just in case.

"What, and they pay three hundred quid even if you lose?"

"Yeah. Win or lose, that's what you get. Three hundred quid." He leans back and grins at me. He can probably tell from the look on my face he's already reeled me in. But it still sounds a bit too good to be true.

"So where do these fights take place?" I say, picking up my sandwich. I bite down on it hard to make sure the tomato doesn't fly out again.

"In a barn."

"Where?"

"That's a secret."

"Well how am I supposed to get there if I don't know where it is?"

"So you're interested then?"

"Dunno. Maybe. I'd need to know a bit more about it first."

"I can take you to one of the fights, if you like? Then if you're up for it I'll introduce you to the boss and you can take it from there."

"So what's in it for you?"

He flashes his teeth again. "What, you mean other than having a pretty girl on my arm for the evening?"

Christ, what a fucking slimeball. Does he really think lines like that actually work on women? I smile. "Yeah, apart from that."

"I get a finder's fee. That's what I was doing in the gym, looking for fresh talent. I reckon you'd be a natural, certainly better than those two clowns in the ring. They were just shite."

I laugh. "Yeah well, you're not wrong there. But you haven't even seen me fight, have you?" I show him my fists. "You fancy going a few rounds, see how good I *really* am?"

"Nah," he says. He leans back and smiles. "I'm a lover, not a fighter." Christ, there he goes again. He certainly loves *himself*, that's for sure.

"So are you paying for dinner then, lover boy?"

His grin falls. He looks around for the waitress. She's

behind the counter wiping cups out with a dirty towel. "Well actually," he says, barely a whisper when he turns back to me, "I were just going to do a runner."

I smile and shake my head. "Nah, fuck that. I'm knackered from my workout in the gym, I don't fancy having to leg it. Tell you what, I'll pay the bill. You can pay me back when you've got the money."

"Sounds good to me," he says, the grin back in place. "There's a fight this Saturday, I'll pay you back then if you come with me. Give me your address and I'll pick you up in my motor."

"What, you've got a car?"

"Yeah, a Cortina." He says this like it's a fucking Rolls Royce or something, and I can't help smiling. He leans forward, waiting for an answer from me. "So what's your address then?"

"I'll meet you outside the chippy on Sandalwood Road. What time's the fight start?"

"Eight o'clock. It'll take about half an hour to get there, so be there at half-seven?"

"Yeah, will do."

Half an hour to get there? That means it must be pretty far away. Say an average fifty miles an hour once you get out of town, that makes it at least twenty miles away. And if it's in a barn it must be in the countryside somewhere, so it shouldn't be too hard to figure out where it is.

"Right, well," I say. I stand up and stretch my arms. "I'm gonna get off then. I'll see you on Saturday, yeah?"

I go to the till and pay the waitress. It turns out Dave was on his second plate of egg and chips when I arrived so it costs a bit more than I expected it to. When I turn to leave, Dave's standing behind me and I almost bump into him.

"You still haven't told me your name," he says.

"Abby."

"Cool. I'll see you on Saturday then, Abby."

3

"What time do you call this?"

That's my boss, Mr fucking Blunt, the rhyming slang manager of the burger joint I work at. Sarcastic bastard, he knows full well what time it is, it's ten past nine. So I'm a bit late, big fucking deal. Better late than not turn up at all, yeah? I could've easily took another day off sick, Mr Cunt wouldn't be able to do fuck all about it.

But instead of being grateful I've dragged my arse into work he'd rather moan about me being late. It's not like I haven't got a good excuse either. My mum didn't come home last night, and my dad was frantic this morning. Said he's worried sick about her, but more likely he's wondering who's going to do the shopping, cooking and cleaning for him.

"Sorry Mr Blunt, it won't happen again."

"Yes well, young lady, you see that it doesn't. There's four million people who would do anything to have your job, and don't you forget that."

As if he would ever let me. Everyone else I was at school with is on what they laughingly call training schemes now, doing jobs just as shitty as mine, except they don't even get paid for it. Thank fuck for the anti-obesity lobby that got fast food joints excluded from that particular scheme, yeah?

Blunt flounces off to his office, no doubt to write a report about me being late to send to head office, and I force my mouth into the regulation happy-face expression when a customer approaches the counter.

"Yes sir, how may I serve you this fine day?"

They make me say that, it's in the staff handbook and it's a sacking offence if I don't. I've said it that many times now I don't even smirk when I say it anymore. I just play it deadpan, like I actually fucking mean it.

The man, a big fat bastard in a suit with grease stains down his shirt and tie, scowls at me. "Big Mac triple cheeseburger, large fries, and a diet Coke," he says.

"Certainly, sir. Will you be dining here or would you like them to go?" That's another one from the staff handbook. As if stuffing your face with grease-and-gristle-burgers could be classed as dining, for fuck's sake. Mr Blunt even refers to the plastic seats and tables as 'the restaurant' if you can believe that?

"To go," he says. "And make it quick, I've got an important appointment to get to."

"Certainly, sir, no problem."

The customer is always right, apparently. Even when they're an ignorant fucking cunt like this one. I resist the urge to curtsy, and make my way to the serving hatch. Colin's on the griddles today. He only works part time, two days a week, he's at college the rest of the week doing a course in car mechanics. He's a decent enough bloke, but with all those spots and boils his face looks like someone's taken a lump hammer to him. Put it this way, it's not by accident he works in the kitchen, hidden away from the customers. No fucker would want to eat here otherwise, they'd be too busy puking on the floor.

"Big Mac triple cheeseburger and large fries," I yell through the hatch. "Make it a special, extra quick."

Colin grins at me and sticks his finger up his nose, twirls it about in there. I take a cardboard cup and pour out a diet Coke, put the plastic lid on and shove a straw through the hole while I wait for the rest of the order.

"One Big Mac triple cheeseburger, extra special, and one large fries," Colin says, passing me a tray through the serving hatch. I smile when I take it, this one genuine rather than painted on. I put the diet Coke on the tray and take it to the lard-arse standing by the counter. He's looking at his watch, as if he's been fucking timing me or something.

"Here you are, sir, enjoy your breakfast and have a nice day." Guess where that line of pure fucking bollocks comes from?

He grunts and takes out his wallet, hands me a ten pound note. I ring it up in the till, pushing the buttons with the right pictures on them, and give him the change the till says he should get. He takes a bite from his burger and turns to leave. Colin watches through the serving hatch, and we both laugh when we look at each other.

"What are you two laughing at?" Sally says, walking out of the toilets with a mop and bucket.

"The bloke who just left, we gave him a special."

Sally smiles and shakes her head. "Fucking hell Abby, if Blunt the Cunt catches you doing that he'll have both your arses on the grill."

"Nah, fuck him. He's busy in his office, wanking off to animal porn. Anyway, we've got to do something to relieve the boredom, haven't we? So are you all right then, Sally? Did you miss me yesterday?"

"Oh, were you not in then? Can't say that I noticed."

"Very funny. I just pissed myself laughing."

"Someone *did* miss you though."

"Oh yeah? Who's that then?"

Sally shrugs. "Dunno, he didn't give a name. Just asked for you, then when I said you weren't in he said he'd call back another day."

"What did he want?"

"Well duh. He wanted you, of course."

"What did he look like?"

"A fat bloke in his thirties. Nice clothes, no grease stains down them, so not like the usual bunch we get in here."

I mentally tick off the fat men I know, trying to work out who it might be. The nice clothes and lack of grease stains rules my dad out straight away, and I can't think of anyone else who would come here looking for me.

"So where were you yesterday then?" Sally asks.

"At home, sick."

"What, sick of work you mean?"

I laugh. "Yeah, something like that."

* * *

At knocking off time I'm first through the door. Blunt looks at his watch and scowls at me. Fuck him, I've done my sentence for the day, now it's my time. I go down to the gym and spend half an hour punching his fucking face in, at least in my head. One day I'll do it for real and wipe the floor with that sarcastic smug bastard, but for now the punch-bag makes a good enough substitute.

The sweat's pouring down me now, and my arms are tired, so I call it a day and towel myself down in the changing room.

"See you, Al," I say as I leave. Big Al grunts his farewell and I make my way home.

Dad's watching Countdown when I get there, and when he turns toward me his eyes are all red and puffy. The scars on his wrists, the result of an accident at the park when I was a little kid, look inflamed. Must be his allergies playing up again, but it's his own fault for not taking his antihistamines.

"Your mum's still not back yet," dad says. His voice is croaky, like he's got a sore throat or something. Maybe he's getting a cold. He'd better not give it to me.

I slump down on the settee and sigh. "Did you have another argument?"

Dad shakes his head. "No. I don't think so, anyway. I was watching telly when she went to work, Bargain Hunt was on. You know I like that one."

"And you haven't heard anything from her since? She hasn't phoned or nothing?" Dad shakes his head again.

"Did you phone her work and ask if she's there?"

"Don't know where that is."

Oh for fuck's sake. How can he not know where his own wife works? Yeah well, I don't know where she works either, just that it's some factory or other. But there's never been any reason for me to know, has there?

"Have you told the police?" I ask.

"What for?"

"What for? She's been missing for two days now, what do you think what for?"

"I don't want no coppers in my house," he says. He scratches his fingernails up and down his arm. They leave white lines criss-crossing the scars on his wrist.

"Well go down to the station then if you don't want them here."

"Can you do it, Abigail? You know I don't like coppers."

Yeah well, I'm not too keen on them myself either, but fucking hell this is my mum here. It'll make a change for the Bastards in Blue to do something useful instead of just sitting around on their arses all day watching the CCTV cameras looking for an easy collar to pull.

"Tell you what," I say. "If we've not heard anything from her by tomorrow I'll go down there after work. Have you had anything to eat yet?"

"No, your mum's not here is she?"

I shake my head and sigh. Fucking lazy bastard, I bet he hasn't moved from that chair since I went to work this morning. "So what do you want for tea?"

"Dunno. What is there?"

Well how the fuck should I know? Mum usually does all the cooking. I get up and go to have a look in the kitchen. There's not much in the cupboards, just a couple of Pot Noodles, a box of Oxo, and half a bag of sugar. My mum's peppermint teabags are conspicuous by their absence, that's the one thing she always keeps well stocked. There's half a loaf in the breadbin, lying open on its side with a few stale slices hanging out. I push them back in and seal it up. I look in the fridge but there's fuck all in there either; three eggs, some margarine, half a pint of milk that's starting to smell, and something green and furry on a plate that could literally be anything.

Scrambled eggs is the logical choice, but I can't be arsed making that so I reach for one of the Pot Noodles. I put the kettle on and grind the dried noodles up with a fork while I wait for it to boil. I don't bother stirring them before I take them in for dad, he can do that himself. The Channel Four news is on, so it's a while before he looks at what I've put down on the arm of his chair.

"Pot Noodle?" he says. "Isn't there anything else?"

"That's all I could find, if you don't want it I'll take it away."

"I didn't say I don't want it," he says, and grabs hold of the pot so I can't take it off him.

"You need to go down to the shops, dad. There's hardly any food at all in the house."

Dad stirs his Pot Noodle with the fork I left in it. "Your mum'll do that when she gets back." He shovels some noodles into his mouth, then spits them back into the pot. "Ow, that's too hot." He blows on the surface of the noodles, then looks at me. "You not having anything, Abigail?"

"I'm going out in a bit, I'll get something then."

"Where are you going?" he asks.

"Just out."

"Oh. But you're coming back later?"

"Of course I am, why wouldn't I?"

"Dunno. Just wondered, that's all."

4

I'm sitting in The Black Swan, waiting for Shaz to turn up. It's still early, and Shaz is always late anyway, so I've got a bit of time to kill. I sip my first Guinness of the night and play Angry Robots on my phone while I wait.

I look up when I hear the door open, and see a bunch of loud-mouthed hooray henrys pile in. I can tell they're already pretty tanked up by the way they sway from side to side while they stand at the bar waiting to be served. They've probably been drinking all day, judging by the state of them.

They give the barmaid a bit of stick, calling her a 'fucking dyke' when she refuses to give one of them a kiss, but she takes it in her stride like a true fucking professional. If it were me I would've just fucking glassed the cunt.

One of them pays for all the drinks, some sort of fucking cocktails would you believe? All multi-coloured shite with little umbrellas sticking out of the top. They look around for somewhere to sit and pose with them, and one catches my eye and smiles. I fold my arms and glare back, but he doesn't take the hint. He walks over and sits down opposite me, puts his lime-green drink down on the table.

"Is anyone sitting here?" he asks.

I shrug and pick up my phone, go back to shooting robots out of a canon. "Just some fucking posh cunt with a glass of snot."

"Ooh, a feisty one. I like a challenge."

The others watch from the bar for a while, sipping their drinks through straws like a bunch of kids at a jelly and ice cream party watching a clown perform. Then they glance at each other and stagger over, fencing me in on all sides when they sit down around the table. The stink of deodorant coming from them makes me gag. Give me the honest smell of sweat and toil any day over this fucking girly-man stench.

"Who's your friend, Tarquin?" one asks. He's a tall, lanky fucker with a massive nose and a pigeon chest. He's got that posh cunt accent with a nasal twang to it that grates on your nerves and makes you want to smack him one just to shut him up.

"I don't know, Kevin. She looks like a Brenda to me. What do you think, Stephen?"

The one called Stephen looks at me, then ducks under the table to look at my legs. I snap them shut. I wouldn't want him spunking all over the inside of his nice trousers, would I? What would his mummy have to say about that?

"She certainly looks like a Brenda to me," he announces. "The red knickers are a dead giveaway."

"So where are you from then, Brenda?" Tarquin asks.

I put my phone away, down the rest of my Guinness, and stand up to leave. I've had enough of these fucking pricks, it's time to go somewhere else.

"Shift," I say. I jerk my thumb at the lanky bastard when he doesn't move out of my way. He just sits there gormless as fuck, staring up at me, so I grab a handful of suit and show him my fist. "Fucking move, you cunt."

The sudden look of fear on his face is fucking priceless. He shuffles his chair back and I barge past, ever so accidentally knocking his girly pink drink over with my elbow. He watches it drip onto the floor, but he doesn't say anything.

"Where are you going, Brenda?"

It's that Tarquin cunt again. He stands up, tries to block my way. I get this sudden urge to boot him in the bollocks, but then I notice the barmaid is watching. I can't afford to get barred from another pub, there's not many left now I can still drink in and I quite like the peaceful atmosphere in The Black Swan. When it's not full of fucking spoilt rich bastard mummy's boys like these, anyway.

I look Tarquin up and down and curl my top lip up into a sneer. "What's it to you like, you fucking ponce."

He laughs, more like a piggy snort than anything else, and that winds me up even more. "Chillax, Brenda, I'm just being friendly. Here, let me buy you a drink." He reaches into an inside pocket and pulls out a leather wallet with gold embossed initials on it, waves it in my face. "Some sort of black stuff you were drinking, I believe?"

I swat the wallet out of my face with the back of my hand and he flinches and drops it. I puff myself up, stretch up onto my toes so we're the same height, and position my face inches away from his. "Listen carefully, you cunt," I say slowly. "Just so that we're fucking clear. If you talk to me again I will fucking deck you. The only reason you're still standing now is because I'm in a good mood. You fuck with me again and that will change. Got it?" He nods. "Good. Now move out of the fucking way and let me past."

Tarquin stands to one side and gestures at the opening with his hand, like he's a fucking gentleman letting me on the bus first or something. I want to smack this cunt real bad, wipe that smug fucking grin off his face, but the barmaid is still watching so I just walk out without another word. I hear one of them say "Rough totty" as I open the door, followed by peels of laughter.

Outside I punch the door and look around for something to kick, but there's never a drunk around when you need one. I think about waiting around outside, then laying into them when they leave to see if they'll piss themselves, but that would just be a waste of good drinking time.

Fuck it, I'll go down to The Black Bull. It's rough as fuck in there, but at least I'll be among my own kind of people. Tarquin and his gang of ponces wouldn't last five seconds in there. It used to be a skinhead hangout when my mum and dad were my age, and it's always had a bit of a bad reputation ever since. When I first started going out on the piss with Shaz my mum warned me to stay well away from that place. Said she used to go out with the landlord there when she was my age and he was a right bastard to her. Reckons he smacked her in the face when she found out he was two-timing her.

So of course The Black Bull was the first pub me and Shaz ever went in. Just to see what mum's old boyfriend looks like, yeah? The way she always goes on about him I expected some sort of fucking monster. He's a bit rough-looking for an old geezer, not someone I'd expect my mum to go for, but he seems sound enough to me.

That first time at The Black Bull was a bit of a let down if I'm honest. Not one single fight the whole time we were there, and every fucker in there was at least twice my age. I did meet a bloke there, so it wasn't a complete waste of time. He worked on a construction site or something, and we had a drunken bunk up round the back at closing time. Built like a brick fucking shithouse he was, muscles the size of footballs, but his cock was a bit of a let down.

I send Shaz a text to let her know about the change of plan. I don't bother telling her about the ponces, I'll save that for when I see her. She'll only want to smack them around, and I can't be bothered with that tonight. I just want to get pissed up and have a good time. I'm not even looking for a shag, never mind a punch up with a bunch of fucking toffs.

There's a bald guy in his early fifties standing outside The Black Bull, puffing away on a cigarette. "All right, darling," he says in a gruff voice as I walk past. I've seen him here plenty of times, so I nod and smile. I think he's one of the old-time regulars or something, I know he's a mate of the landlord anyway, so he's one of the people you don't piss off if you want to carry on drinking at The Black Bull.

I push through the door. There's something rowdy playing on the jukebox and the place is half full of people. There's all ages in tonight, from youngsters hovering around the pool table to more bald blokes in their fifties, like the one outside, sat at a table near the door. I look around for Shaz, but she's not here yet.

The landlord nods toward me when I approach the bar. He walks over with a limp.

"Pint of Guinness," I yell over the music. He nods again and picks up a glass, fills it from a bottle. He's got tattoos on his arms, everything from bulldogs to dragons all mingling together to cover every inch of skin. On one side of his neck there's a love-heart with a blood-soaked dagger stabbed through it with the name Mandy in a scroll underneath.

He puts the Guinness down on a soaking wet bar towel and holds out his hand, I give him the money and wait for my change. The baldy from outside must've finished his fag because he's walking toward the bar when I turn to leave. He nods at me, I nod back. I can feel him staring at me as I walk away.

"Now then Trog, you fat bastard," I hear him say to the landlord. "We having a fucking lock-in or what?"

I take my drink to an empty table and sit down, watch the door for Shaz. It's not long before some chancer comes over on the pull.

"Hi," he shouts, and sits down opposite me. He's not too shabby looking, so I don't tell him to fuck off straight away. "Abby, right?"

I look at him a bit closer, wondering where he knows me from, and nod.

"Remember me?"

I take a sip of my Guinness and study him over the rim of the glass. "No, sorry," I say, and shake my head.

"It's Bob," he says. He points at his chest and smiles.

"We were at school together."

"Oh yeah, I remember."

But I don't really. Bob? Bob who? But he starts going on about some of the teachers, and those fucking bastards I definitely do remember. I laugh when he recounts the tale of when Mr Jenkins flipped out and started crying because we were all making a humming noise and he couldn't work out where the fuck it was coming from. If this Bob, whoever he is, knew about what we did to Old Jenkins, then he must have been in the same class as me? So who the fuck is he then? I think back and start to tick off all the boys' names in my head while he prattles on.

It's Shaz who fills in the blanks for me when she arrives. "Bobby Tatlock, fucking hell you've lost a lot of weight haven't you?"

The guy beams at Shaz and rises to his feet, gives her a hug. This startles Shaz, and she gives me a funny look over his shoulder. She breaks away, holds him at arm's length, and looks him up and down. She grins. "You're looking good there, Tatty."

Fatty Tatty! No wonder I didn't recognise the cunt, he's about a third of the size he was when we were at school. He must have gained a lot of confidence too, there's no way he would've been brave enough to do anything like that back then. He always just sat at the back of the class, never saying a word to anyone. He was probably the only lad in the entire fucking school who never got to finger Shaz in the nearby woods at some point or other too. In fact she probably would've fucking decked him if he ever so much as looked at her when we were at school. But here she is now, all over him like he's a fucking stud or something.

"You getting the drinks in then, Tatty?" Shaz asks. She sits down and gives me a wink.

Tatty nods. "Um... yeah, sure. What do you want?"

"Double Pernod for me."

Tatty looks at me and raises his head. I drain my glass and ask for another Guinness. He wanders off to the bar and I turn to Shaz.

"What's with the fucking Pernod? You usually drink lager."

She shrugs. "That's just when I'm paying for it. I always go for Pernod when someone else is picking up the tab."

Tatty comes back from the bar with our drinks and puts them down in the middle of the table.

"Cheers Tatty," Shaz says. She picks up her double Pernod and downs it in one gulp. She puts the empty glass down and looks up at Tatty expectantly.

Like a daft cunt, he says, "You want another one of those?" Shaz nods, and off he goes again. I shake my head at Shaz. Shaz laughs.

"Fuck it, why not?" she says. "He did offer, it's not like I had to twist his fucking arm."

"Poor kid, he's probably as skint as we are."

I tell Shaz about the posh cunts in The Black Swan, and like I expected she wants to go down there and smack the fuck out of them.

I shake my head. "Nah, they'll be long gone by now."

"Who's that then?" Tatty says, back with another Pernod for Shaz. She sips this one, so Tatty sits down next to her. His wallet gives a sigh of relief.

I shrug. "Nobody important. But that reminds me," I say to Shaz, "I met a guy the other day."

Shaz sits up and leans over the table. "Oh yeah? What's he like?"

"He's a skinhead, but he seems quite nice."

"A fucking skinhead? Can't see him having much money then."

"Oh, I don't know. He's got a car, so he must be pretty well off, yeah? Petrol costs a fucking bomb."

Shaz's eyes widen. "A car? Fuck me, he must be loaded. So what does he do for a living?"

"Dunno, I didn't ask. He's taking me out on Saturday, to some fight or something."

"What about The Meat Market?"

My eyes flick toward Tatty, but he doesn't seem to have picked up on anything. I give Shaz a look that I hope says 'watch what you fucking say while he's here' and take a sip of Guinness before I reply.

"We'll have to skip it this week, yeah?"

Shaz folds her arms and glares at me.

* * *

It's closing time and Shaz is pissed out of her fucking head, slumped over the table with her head resting on her arms. She got Tatty buying her drinks all night like a daft cunt, fuck knows what was going on in his head. He probably thought it was the start of some big fucking romance or something, but Shaz played him good and proper, using him as a source of free Pernod. She hardly even spoke to the guy, except when she was telling him she needed another drink. I hope he's not on the dole, he must've spent at least twenty-five quid on her tonight. He fucked off at half-ten, said he needed to catch the last bus. Shaz didn't even say goodbye.

I nudge Shaz's arm with my elbow. She looks up at me as if she doesn't know where the fuck she is. "Whu..?" she says. She sits up and rubs her eyes. She looks around for her drink, but the landlord's already whisked it away along with all the empty glasses we've been accumulating through the night. "What the fuck time is it?"

I take out my phone and stare at the screen long enough to get it into focus. "Ten past twelve."

Shaz frowns and shakes her head, like she's trying to

get her thoughts sorted into the right order. The landlord glares at us, it won't be long before he comes over to turf us out. The old guys at the table by the door have got fresh drinks though, so it looks like they get preferential treatment. They're arguing about some band or other I've never heard of, whether they were racist or not. It seems to be getting quite heated, with a lot of fists banging down on the table top.

"Fuck me," Shaz says, "I feel rough as fuck."

"Yeah well, it's time to get fucked off home. You coming?"

Shaz nods, and pulls herself up to her feet with the help of the table. "I need a piss first, you coming?"

"Nah, don't need one. I'll wait here for you."

Shaz staggers into the toilet and I load up Angry Robots while I wait. But I can't get my fingers coordinated enough to play it properly, so I give up and put the phone back in my pocket.

"We off then?" I say when Shaz gets back. She nods, and we stagger to the door together.

"Night," the landlord says from the bar. Shaz raises her hand and waves. I nod at him. One day I'll tell him who my mum is, see if he remembers her. Not tonight though.

I look at the three old-timers sat by the door, envious as fuck as I watch them drink their lager. "Fuck off Don, you nazi bastard," one shouts. His nose is bent out of shape and he's got scars all over his face. He looks a right fucking cunt, someone even I wouldn't want to mess with, but the guy he's arguing with doesn't back down. "Fucking commie," I hear him reply as we walk through the door. The landlord locks and bolts it behind us.

Shaz bends over and pukes into the gutter. A couple of passers-by point and laugh when the liquid vomit bounces off the road and splatters up her legs. Shaz doesn't seem to notice, which is just as well for the passers-by because if she did they wouldn't be laughing for long when she smacked them in their mouths.

I wait for Shaz to finish spewing, and take out my phone to order a taxi. While I'm dialling the number Shaz announces she's fucking starving and wants some chips. Now that she mentions it I wouldn't mind some myself. There's a chip shop just down the road, at the other side of the market, so we make our way there, arm in arm, leaning against each other for support.

There's the usual long queue you always get at fast food joints when everyone gets turfed out of the pubs at the same time and has the exact same idea as everyone else. Someone points at one of the goldfish swimming around in a tank by the side of the till and says he wants that one in batter. The old woman in a white hat and overalls behind the counter smiles politely, as if she's never heard that one before.

I buy a tray of chips, Shaz gets chips and gravy. She gets a free plastic spoon with little prongs on the end of it, I have to make do with a flimsy wooden fork. We're walking out of the shop eating our chips when I hear a voice from the other side of the road.

"I say Tarquin, isn't that your rough totty over there?"

"It certainly is, Nigel. And look, she even has a friend for you. What do you say we go over and give them a tug?"

I look over, it's two of those posh cunts from The Black Swan. I ignore them and carry on walking, looking for a wall to sit on while I have my supper.

"Hey Brenda, wait up."

I hear footsteps running behind me and I stop and spin toward them. Shaz must have heard them as well because she turns to face them too.

"Who's this pair of cunts then?" Shaz asks.

The two ponces slow their pace when they see we're waiting for them.

"Two of them posh fuckers from The Black Swan," I tell Shaz.

I look around to see how many cameras are covering the area around the chip shop. There's a few private ones bolted to the walls of nearby shops and houses, but those are only interested in their own security so they won't have the right angle to take in the whole street. There's no police cameras, it's too far away from the town centre for those and it's a low-rent area of town anyway so they probably don't care about any of the people who live or work here.

"Here, hold my chips for me," I say, and hand Shaz my polystyrene chip tray. She balances it in the palm of her free hand and grins at me.

"Don't take too long about it, my chips are going cold," she says.

I nod and walk toward Tarquin.

"Hello Brenda, couldn't keep away from us, could you?" Tarquin says, a smug grin on his face. He points at Shaz. "Who's your cute friend over there?"

I close the gap between us in two strides, my fists clenched and ready. He doesn't see it coming. One second he's standing there grinning at me, the next he's lying on the floor clutching his mouth and looking up at me in shock. His mate stares at me wide-eyed as if he can't believe what's just happened. You'd think smarmy bastards like these two would be used to people punching their fucking faces in by now.

I straddle Tarquin and drop down onto his stomach with my knees. His head jerks up and his face goes purple as he struggles for breath. I lean forward and smack him in the mouth again a couple of times. His head jerks to one side and blood flies out of his mouth. There's no loose teeth in the blood though, which is a shame. I clasp my hands together and give him a hammer-blow in the ear and he cries out with this fucking pathetic-sounding wail like a kicked puppy.

I feel something wet on my ankles and stand up to see what it is. The dirty fucking bastard has only gone and fucking pissed on me hasn't he. Well that does it, yeah? I'd just about vented my fucking rage on the cunt, now it's boiling up inside me again. I lift my boot and stamp down on his leg. He cries out again and rolls himself into a ball. I kick him up the arse a few times and his body jerks forward each time. Shaz joins me, a tray of chips held in each hand, and kicks out at the hands covering the bastard's face. She grins at me while she kicks away at him, and I stand back to watch.

I remember his mate, and spin around to face him. He's trembling by the side of the road, like it's the middle of fucking winter or something. His eyes are wide and staring, and when I walk toward him he backs away. I lunge forward and he screams like a fucking girl in a 1970s horror movie. I grab him round the waist, bend my head down, and push him over. He falls flat on his arse, I land on top of him, and his head cracks back onto the pavement with a dull thud. I raise my fists to pummel his face, but he's already unconscious. I give him a smack in the mouth anyway, something for him to remember me by, and head back to Shaz to get my chips. All this exercise has made me fucking starving.

I seem to have drawn a bit of a crowd. People are staring, open-mouthed like strangled goldfish. One of them seems to be enjoying the spectacle though, and he gives me a round of applause. I smile, and bow in his direction. My tray of chips is perched on the kerb, next to Shaz's chips and gravy. I walk over and pick them up, stuff a handful in my mouth. I'm too hungry to bother with the little wooden fork.

Shaz rolls Tarquin onto his back and checks his pockets.

She pulls out a wallet and hands it to me. I flip it open with one hand, it's stuffed full of money and credit cards. I put it in my pocket and get another handful of chips. Shaz walks over to Nigel, pulls out his wallet and waves it at me, grinning like she's just won the jackpot.

"We'd best get fucked off," I say, "one of those cunts will have probably called the coppers by now."

Shaz looks at the small crowd of wide-eyed gawpers outside the chip shop. She shrugs. "Yeah, you're probably right."

We cut through an alleyway round the back of the chip shop to get off the main road, and take a few turns at random until we end up in a run-down residential area. I pull out my phone and order a taxi, giving the name of the road. The bored-sounding Asian guy on the other end of the phone says it'll be here in fifteen minutes.

We sit on a wall and share out the money while we wait. The credit cards are no use to us, they're too easy to trace if you use them, so we drop them down the drain along with the wallets.

I can hear sirens in the distance. I feel sorry for anyone who's daft enough to wait around to give a statement to the police. Their reward for being a good citizen will be a night in the cells while they sober up, followed by relentless grilling in the early hours of the morning when their hangover is at its worst. If they've got any sense they will have scarpered soon after me and Shaz did.

A car pulls up and a young Asian guy looks out at us. "You order mini-cab?" he asks.

I nod, and we jump down off the wall and pile into the back seat, laughing. We've both got lots of extra cash in our pockets when all we were expecting was a good piss up. So it's been a pretty good night out, all things considered.

5

The closer it gets to Saturday the more excited I get. I've never really been out on a proper date with a bloke before, at least not with one I've never even fucked. Yeah, I've had guys coming back for second helpings, taking me to the cinema to live out their fantasy of shagging someone on the back row; or getting naked on top of a multi-story car park or whatever. I've also had guys take me to the pub to show off their latest conquest to their mates. But never anything as romantic as an underground fight in a barn on the outskirts of Homefirth. Yeah, I found out where it is the other night, it took me about ten fucking minutes of looking through Google Maps on my phone. So much for top secret locations, yeah?

Shaz phoned me last night, and tried to talk me out of going to the fight. She made me feel really fucking guilty about not going to The Meat Market with her. Said she needed me to be there, and she couldn't do it by herself. I told her with all the money we've made this week it wouldn't really matter if we skipped it just this once, and promised I'd go with her next week. Then Shaz asked if she could come to the fight with me and Dave instead. I told her it was invite only and that I'd see if I could get her an invite for the next one. I don't know if Dave would mind a plus-one or not, the truth is I just don't want Shaz to be there. Don't get me wrong, I love her to fucking bits, but she's not the best of company when you're out with a guy. She tends to show off and command all their attention, while I just get sidelined into the background.

Saturday morning I wake up early to birds twittering somewhere. I can hear dad snoring away when I walk past his room to the toilet, so I bang down the wooden seat as loud as I can just to pay him back for all the times he's woke me up in the past. I go downstairs in my bunny slippers and nightie trying to make as much noise as possible, and switch on the TV. It's tuned to some boring twaddle, so I change it to one of the music channels and turn up the volume so I can hear it from the kitchen while I have my breakfast.

I had to do a shop the other day, dad couldn't be bothered as usual, so I've stocked the fridge with all the things I like. I take out a peach yoghurt and rip the lid off, lick it clean while I get a spoon from the drawer.

I smile to myself when I hear dad thumping around upstairs. I expect him to be in a mood when he comes down, and I prepare myself for a blazing row, but he seems more miserable than anything else. He turns down the volume on the TV, but doesn't change the channel.

In the absence of an argument I make him a mug of tea and take it in to him. He grunts when I hand it to him, his gaze riveted on the TV. There's some new boy-band prancing around half-naked on the screen, miming along to the words of the song. Dad's cheeks are wet, and I watch a tear roll down one. I get him an antihistamine tablet from the kitchen and he pops it in his mouth without looking at it.

"Are you okay, dad?"

He looks up at me, cradling the mug in both hands. "It's been nearly a week now and we've still not heard nothing."

"I'm sure she's okay. The police would've told us by now if anything had happened to her."

"Yeah but she's not here is she? And you're out at work all day, and then out all hours at night. I'm just stuck here by myself."

"Maybe she just needs a bit of time by herself?"

"What for?"

"Dunno. Don't we all, sometimes?"

I must admit, I'm starting to get a bit worried about

mum too. I can understand her being fed up with dad, he's not exactly easy to live with, but she could've at least let me know she was okay. The police weren't interested when I reported her missing. No real surprise there. They said they would be in touch if anything turned up, which I took to mean if they found any dead bodies matching her description. But since mum was an adult there wasn't much else they could do, they said. In other words, they couldn't be fucking bothered.

I make dad a few sandwiches for later, wrap them in cling-film for him so they'll stay fresh for when he wants them, then go upstairs to get dressed. I take out all my best outfits and lay them down on the bed, trying to decide which one to wear for tonight. What's the dress code for an underground fight in a barn? Nothing too fancy, I'd guess, but I don't want to look like a complete skank. I settle on a short denim skirt and a black top, and put all the other clothes back in the wardrobe. I hang the skirt and top I've chosen on the outside of the wardrobe door so I can change into them later, and put on my tracksuit and trainers.

"Abby, can you make me something to eat?" dad says when he hears me coming down the stairs. There's some gardening programme on the TV, so he must've got bored with the music. Fuck knows why he chose gardening though, all we've got is a concrete yard full of junk. You couldn't even grow weeds out there.

"Yeah, okay."

"What are you doing with yourself today?" dad asks as I walk into the kitchen.

"Dunno, haven't really thought about it. I'm going out tonight though."

"Huh. You're always going out," I hear him grumble. "Can't you spend the day here instead? It's not like you've got work today or anything."

Christ, I can't think of anything worse than staying here all day with him. I know he only wants someone to feed him, but I'm his fucking daughter not his wife. Besides, I need to do something interesting otherwise the day will just drag and it'll seem like forever before I get to the fight.

"I could stay until dinner time, if you like?"

"Well don't put yourself out on my account."

I unwrap his sandwiches and take them to him. He lifts up a crust, peers inside to see what's in them. They must meet his approval because they don't last long. He burps his appreciation and scratches his balls through a hole in the front of his pyjamas.

"Another cup of tea would go down a treat," he says, sniffing his finger.

"Right. Well tell you what, you go and get dressed and I'll make you one, yeah?"

"Can't," he says. "I got sick on my clothes last night, and I don't like the way they smell."

"Well can't you put some clean ones on?"

He shakes his head. "Your mum usually gets my clean clothes out for me."

Oh for fuck's sake. Nobody's that fucking useless, he *has* to be putting it on for attention. "Fine," I say in a tone that I hope conveys my disgust, "I'll go and pick some clothes out for you then, shall I?"

"Thanks, Abigail. Don't know what I'd do without you."

I clump upstairs and walk into his and mum's bedroom. It stinks of acrid vomit, with a faint whiff of stale piss and spunk coming from the unmade bed. I draw the curtains and open the bedroom windows to let a bit of air in, but it doesn't really help much. It's too muggy outside, and there's no wind today. With the light from outside I can see it's not just the crumpled clothes on the floor my dad has been sick on, his duvet is covered in it too.

There's an empty Special Brew can by the side of the

bed. I pick it up and throw it out of the window. It clatters down on something out there and next door's dog starts to bark. It's not long before I hear my neighbour yelling at the dog to shut up.

I open the wardrobe door and look at all the empty coat hangers. My dad's clothes are still in there, but that's about it. A few old dresses my mum got too fat for years ago are at the end of the rail, but everything else of hers is missing. Along with the old suitcase that only ever used to come out at holiday time when I was little and we still went away once a year. Bollocks, wherever the fuck mum is it looks like she's gone there prepared for a long stay. I pick out some clothes for dad, knowing in advance that he'll grumble about them whichever ones I choose, and take them downstairs for him.

"I don't like those, they pinch too much," dad says, but I don't stay around to listen. I go back upstairs to get the dirty washing. I'll put it in the machine and go down to the gym while I wait for it to wash. Hopefully next door won't have started a fire by the time I get back so I can peg it out to dry.

I hope mum comes back soon, I shouldn't have to deal with stuff like this.

6

Saturday night at fucking last, and I'm standing on the corner of Sandalwood Road eating a bag of chips. It's quite windy tonight, and I wish I'd put a pair of thick tights on under the denim skirt because my legs are fucking freezing. I probably should've put a jacket on as well because I've got goosebumps on my arms the size of fucking marbles. Oh well, too late now. Maybe Dave will be a fucking gentleman and wrap a coat around me, but I'm not holding my breath on that one. That sort of bollocks only happens in the movies. I'll be expecting him to sing next.

It's twenty to eight according to my phone, and there's still no sign of the cunt. I got here early so I know I haven't missed him. A car approaches me slowly and pulls up opposite. The tinted passenger-side window rolls down smoothly with a hum, but it's not Dave inside, it's some fucking prick in a suit.

"Are you looking for business?" the prick says, leaning across with his arm draped over the back of the empty passenger seat.

"Fuck off," I yell, and he drives away. Why the fuck do cunts like that always think I'm a prossie?

I finish my chips and ball up the paper, drop-kick it into the street. I rub the goosebumps off my arms and take out my phone, check the time again. If the bastard's stood me up I'll fucking kick his head in the next time I see him.

A car horn blares out, one of those old musical ones that plays the Hitler Has Only Got One Ball tune. Fuck knows what its real name is, but I'm sure you know the one I mean, yeah? You don't tend to hear horns like those much. I don't know why, they sound fucking cool. I look up the street in the direction of the horn and see a dilapidated-looking grey Cortina parked by the side of the road. It's got a tinted windscreen, so I can't see who's inside but there's only really one person it could be so I wave and walk toward it.

The passenger door opens and I look inside to check it's not another fucking sad bastard who needs to pay for a shag. Dave grins out at me, and I get in. There's two other guys in the back seat, two more skinheads. I'm a bit disappointed to see them, I thought it would be just me and Dave. If I'd known there was going to be other guys I would've brought Shaz with me to make up the numbers.

"All right, Abby," Dave says, grinning at me. "Sorry we're a bit late, blame Josh back there. He spilt lager down his shirt and he's a fucking girl so he had to go home and get changed."

"Fuck off," one of the skinheads in the back says, and I guess this is Josh. "It were your fault for driving like a fucking nutter. You should've warned me you were going to drive off like that, I would've waited before I took a swig."

"Fucking traffic light, weren't it," Dave says, "that's what you're supposed to do when there's some cunt on a motorbike trying to cut in front of you."

"Here you go, darling," the other skinhead says, and a can of lager is held through the gap between the front seats. I take it and crack it open, take a long drink to rinse the chip grease from my mouth. "I'm Steve," he adds, and I turn and nod to him.

Dave opens a glove compartment and pulls out some CDs. They're all home-made copies in plastic sleeves, with hand-written marker pen scrawl on them. He picks one out and rams it into the CD player, tosses the others back in the glove compartment. There's a can of lager wedged between his legs like a big metal cock, and he takes a sip from it before he grinds the car into gear. Loud guitar feedback blares out from speakers in the back window, followed by fast drumming, crashing guitars. Then a geezer with a rough voice shouts something about 'your time will come' but it's hard to decipher any of the lyrics even with the skinheads at the back of the car shouting along with them.

Dave revs the engine and the car lurches forward with a screech of tyres, pushing me back in my seat with a jolt. I can see how Josh managed to spill his lager. 'We're off, here we go,' the geezer on the CD shouts. This one's something about London as far as I can make out. Dave looks at me and grins, I check my seatbelt is secure and smile back.

The traffic lights on the edge of town are red, and there's a couple of cars in front of us when we get there. Dave pulls up behind the second car, leaving a big gap. He grips the steering wheel hard and stares unblinking at the red light. As soon as it changes to amber we jerk forward and I'm pushed back in my seat again. Just as I think we're going to crash into the back of the car in front Dave wrenches the steering wheel and we lurch to one side, into the lane for oncoming traffic. I grab onto a handrail above the door to stop myself from tumbling onto Dave's lap. He sounds the musical horn when we zoom past the two cars and narrowly miss an oncoming motorcycle. I can actually see the look of sheer fucking terror on the biker's face just before Dave pulls back onto the right side of the road.

Just outside town we turn left onto a country road. The tyres screech as we take the corner too fast. It's a sixty mile per hour zone, but it's not long before we accelerate up to ninety. The engine's really screaming now, it's almost loud enough to drown out the music, and the whole car is vibrating like fuck.

When the music ends, Dave ejects the CD with one hand while he grips the steering wheel with the other. He tosses the CD into the glove compartment and pulls out another. He holds it up, studies the writing on the label, and discards it. He reaches inside for a different CD. This one must meet his approval because he pushes it into the CD player. More loud shouty music blares out. At a guess that's the only type he's got in there, so I don't see why he's so choosy about which one we listen to. I'm treated to another round of shouted karaoke from the back seat, so the two skinheads back there must approve of his new selection.

There's a thirty miles per hour sign coming up in the distance, but Dave doesn't seem to be in any hurry to slow down. *Homeforth welcomes careful drivers*, another sign says. Underneath it says *Please check your speed*. We've passed the thirty sign before Dave slams on the brakes and I'm catapulted forward. The seatbelt digs into my chest. I feel a thud against the back of my seat, probably one of the skinheads not bracing himself in time because it's soon followed by a string of obscenities aimed at the driver. Dave laughs and tells him to fuck off.

There's a sharp bend in the road at the entrance to the village, and the car lurches to one side when we take it. We pass a row of boarded up shops, then turn right at a T-junction onto a dirt track. The car bumps up and down over potholes in the road, and I need to grab onto the door handle to steady myself.

There's high, overgrown hedges on both sides of the road, you can't see fuck all apart from them and the road. Dave slows down, peering through the window at the hedge on my side. We come to a small gap in the hedge, barely big enough for a car to drive through, and he pulls up alongside it. You would never have guessed it was there from the road unless you knew where to look. Dave does a seven-point turn on the narrow road, lines the car up with the gap in the hedge, and we drive through. Branches slap against the windows on both sides, and we drive into a field with lots of other cars parked in it. He finds a space to park in and switches off the engine, killing the music at the same time.

"You're gonna fucking love this, Abby," Dave says. He turns toward me and grins.

Steve and Josh pile out of the back of the car and slam the doors behind them. They walk away. I get out and look around. The field is full of weeds, with deep, muddy tyre tracks leading back onto the road. In the distance there's a large house with a dilapidated barn at its outskirts, and I see it's the barn the two skinheads are heading for.

I wait for Dave to lock the car and we follow them across the field. Dave drapes an arm around my shoulder, and it takes him a while to fall into step with me so it's not bumping up and down against me. I put my arm around his waist and hook my thumb around one of his braces.

There's a huge, ugly fucker standing by the barn door with a baseball bat in his hand, talking to Steve and Josh. "Who the fuck's this?" he asks, pointing at me.

"All right, Johnno," Dave says. "This is my bird Abby, she's sound."

The ugly fucker scowls at me. "Not really the place to bring a young girly, Davie-boy. You sure she won't faint?"

I clench my fists. Baseball bat or not I'll fucking deck the cheeky bastard for calling me a girly. But Dave moves in front of me before I can take a swing at him.

"Nah, she's tougher than she looks, Johnno. This time next week she'll be one of the fighters."

Johnno looks at me and laughs. "What, a scrawny little bitch like that? Wouldn't last five fucking seconds."

Dave must be able to read my mind because he turns and grabs both my hands by the wrists. "Nah, she's got some serious fucking moves on her," he says, winking at me. "The best I've seen for a long time."

I can't help smiling. He hasn't even seen me fight yet, not properly anyway. Johnno grunts and points toward the barn door with his baseball bat. We all shuffle through the door and there's another ugly fucker with a baseball bat just inside. I mean seriously, they could be fucking twins or something, yeah?

"All right, Baz," Dave says, though fuck knows how he can tell them apart.

"All right, Davie-boy," Baz says, looking at me. "Who's the bird?"

"This is Abby, she's sound."

Ugly Fucker Two looks at me and shrugs. Dave pulls out a wallet and hands him a fistful of tenners. The money disappears into a belt around his waist and he stands to one side to let us through. Steve and Josh are about to follow when he bars their way with the baseball bat.

"Get your money out, lads. He only paid for him and the bird, not you two."

There's a bit of grumbling at that, and Josh calls Dave a tight get, but they pay up in the end and get ushered through the door to join us.

You can practically taste the fucking testosterone in this place, the air is so thick with the stink of stale blood and sweat. And the heat! Fuck me, it's boiling in here. The barn is packed with people, almost all of them men, though I do see the odd rough-looking woman among them. In one corner there's a table selling something. There's a lot of money changing hands, but I can't see what it is people are buying. Another table is selling beer, judging by the people walking away from it with cans in their hands. I wonder if they've got any Guinness. That lager I had on the way here tasted like fucking gnat's piss and I could do with a proper drink to wash the taste away.

Against the far wall of the barn there's a large cage,

about sixteen feet times twelve feet. A crowd mills around it, but the cage itself is empty. Dave grabs my hand and pulls me through the crowd, barging his way toward the cage. We get jostled by sweaty blokes as we squeeze through, and we're pushed back a few times by people who refuse to make way for us, but we make it to the front eventually. The back of the cage has a door that opens up to the outside of the barn, and there are cameras mounted on the bars, pointing inside. There's a camera covering each side of the cage, and another mounted on top for an aerial view. The floor of the cage is just bare wooden floorboards, no canvas covering, not even any paint or varnish. Just raw planks of wood nailed onto a make-shift stage that raises the cage a few inches from the ground.

Dave drapes his arm around my shoulder and speaks into my ear, "What do you think of it?"

"It's a bit different to a boxing ring."

Dave laughs. But before he can say anything else the cage door opens and a young woman wearing nothing but a pair of red knickers walks through carrying a cardboard placard. She parades around the cage holding the placard above her head. Her tits bounce up and down to loud cheers from the crowd. 'Big Tone versus The Black Marauder' the placard says, in large, bold lettering. She holds it in front of one of the cameras for a few seconds, and then flounces back through the door.

A man storms through the door, face like fucking thunder, and struts around spitting through the cage bars into the crowd. He's stripped to the waist and his overly-muscled body is covered in scars, like he's been in a knife fight with fucking Wolverine or something. His nose is crooked, and when he snarls in my direction I see he's hardly got any teeth left, just three tombstones at the top and a couple at the bottom. They're a fucking weird shape too, more triangular than normal teeth, more like dog's teeth than anything else. He stamps across to one corner of the cage and beats his chest like a gorilla. The crowd yells abuse at him, he yells back.

Another guy strides through the cage door. This one's a half-caste so I guess he must be The Black Marauder. Except he's a lot taller than the gorilla who arrived first, so he could just as easily be Big Tone. This one's also stripped to the waist, and his arms are like fucking tree trunks. The cage door is slammed behind him, and both men scream abuse at each other.

"What are the rules?" I shout to Dave, but he doesn't hear me over the roar of the crowd. I'm pressed up against the side of the cage, I can barely move from the pressure behind me as everyone tries to get closer to the action. Fuck it, I'm sure I'll figure it out once it gets started.

A bell rings somewhere and they fly at each other, their fists a flurry as they lash out. The half-caste ducks down and grabs the white guy around the waist, tries to pull him to the ground. The white guy returns the embrace and brings a knee up into the half-caste's bollocks. The half-caste must have some sort of protection down there, he doesn't even flinch. He lets go of the white guy's waist and pummels his fists down on top his head, like he's playing the fucking bongos or something. The white guy lowers his head and clamps his teeth over the half-caste's shoulder. He bites down and draws blood, shakes his head like a dog. The half-caste cries out and kicks him in the shins, grabs hold of his ears to try and prise him off his shoulder.

The sight of blood makes the crowd surge forward, shouting, and I'm crushed against the bars. I can hardly fucking breathe, the pressure is that great. Some sweaty bruiser pushes his way between me and Dave and grabs hold of the cage bars with both hands. He shouts racial abuse at the half-caste. What a fucking charmer. He's wearing a string vest, and acrid-stinking sweat pours down from his hairy armpits. My face is only inches away from one of his armpits, and it's making my fucking eyes water but I can't get away from him.

The two guys in the cage are in another embrace, trying to spin each other around. Their legs dart in and out in an attempt to trip each other over. There's blood pouring out of a nasty-looking gash in the half-caste's shoulder. It drips down his arm and onto the floorboards. The white guy roars and surges forward, pushes the half-caste up to the cage bars. The people standing at that side of the cage let go of the bars and try to step back just before the half-caste slams into them, but the crowd behind don't give them enough room to move. The cage shudders with the impact. You can tell from the look on the half-caste's face he's in fucking agony, but he manages to get another kick in when the white guy lets go and swings his fist back. He ducks down to his knees just in time, and the white guy punches the cage bars. There's a loud crack and he screams out in pain. The half-caste bounces up like a coiled spring and smacks him in the mouth. He stumbles back and the half-caste runs forward, head down, and nuts him in the stomach.

The crowd are going fucking wild now. The sweaty fucker in the string vest doesn't seem very happy. I'm guessing he wants the white guy to win, but just about everyone else is egging the half-caste on and baying for blood.

The white guy isn't down yet, but he doesn't look like he's far from it. He staggers to one side and lashes out with his uninjured fist, but none of his blows land with any real impact. There's blood pouring from his mouth, down his chin and onto his chest. Unless he pulls something out of the hat soon it's only a matter of time now. The half-caste knows it too. He grins as he dodges back and forth, lashing out with those huge fists of his. But he's getting too confident. He's going all out on the attack and leaving his defences wide open. I see several opportunities where you could take advantage of that, but the white guy just stands there like a fucking punch-bag. He doesn't even bother fighting back, just staggers backwards with each blow.

"Get under his fucking arms," I yell, pointing through the bars of the cage. "Go for his fucking knees, you useless fucking cunt."

The sweaty fucker in the string vest turns and grins at me, like he's found an Aryan sister or something. I scowl back to put him right. It's not about fucking colour, it's about fighting back. You don't just give in when someone's got the upper hand. You look for a weakness in their attack and take advantage of it, and the half-caste is certainly leaving himself wide open for that. If I was in there I know what I'd do in that position, it's just textbook street fighting. Duck down under his fists and yank his knee forward, he'll soon crumple to the ground. Then you can stick the boot in and finish the bastard off.

But fuck knows where this guy learnt his fighting from because he doesn't do any of that. He backs away, tries to get himself a bit of breathing space, but the half-caste won't let him. He closes the gap, jabs out with his fists, and backs him up against the bars. Face, then chest, then side of the head, then face again. The white guy stands there taking it, holding his hands up in surrender.

I expect that to be the end of the fight, game over for the white guy, but the crowd are still roaring for more. The half-caste leans back and launches a kung-fu kick at his opponent's stomach. The white guy doubles over in agony, and gets a knee in the face. His head flies back and cracks against the bars, and his legs give way beneath him. The half-caste kicks him in the head, knocks him onto his side, and grabs his feet. He rolls him onto his back and drags him to the centre of the cage. The white guy doesn't struggle, he just lies there staring up the camera mounted on top of the cage. The half-caste puts his foot on the man's chest and raises both hands above his head. He roars in victory.

But still the crowd aren't satisfied. They cry out for the victor to finish it. Anyone can see he's already won, so what the fuck is there left to finish? The crowd stamp their feet in rhythm. It sounds like an army marching across a bridge in hobnail boots. Fuck knows what they're expecting the half-caste to do, but when he just spits in the white guy's face and walks up to the cage door they all groan in disappointment. The half-caste bangs on the door with his fist, and it's opened. He walks through, and an old man in spectacles makes his way toward the man lying in the centre of the cage.

The crush around me begins to ease as people shuffle away, talking excitedly to each other. I stay to see what happens next. The old man prises the white guy's eyelids open and shines a torch into them. He feels along his arms and legs, presses down on his chest with the palms of his hands.

"Fucking smart, eh?" Dave says in my ear. His arms curl round my waist from behind. His hands slide up to my tits and he squeezes them together.

I squirm myself around to face him and smile. "Yeah, fucking brilliant."

* * *

The last fight of the night is the only women's bout of the evening, and they're even more vicious than the men. Not as vicious as me, of course, but their ferocity takes me by surprise. I was expecting it to be more about light relief and titillation for the men in the audience than anything else. But the way the women lay into each other they definitely mean fucking business. Mind you, that doesn't stop the charmer in the string vest from getting a hard-on and touching himself while he watches them slug each other. Or maybe that's because he's pressed up against me? Dirty fucking bastard, he's older than my dad.

After the fight's over and the crowd around the cage thins out, Dave asks me if I've made my mind up about whether I want to fight or not. He reminds me about the three hundred quid on offer, even if I lose. After seeing the mistakes the men were making I'd already pretty much made my mind up. But it was the women's fight that sealed it for me. The mindless way they went about slamming into each other, the obvious targets they went for to cause maximum pain for their opoponent. A bit of extra protection in the right places and they wouldn't have a fucking clue where to hit me. I'd be walking out of that cage without a fucking scratch, the easiest money I ever made.

"Yeah, I'm in. Where do I sign up?"

Dave grins at me. "We'll hold back until everyone's fucked off, then I'll introduce you to Lonnie. He's the main man."

Sweat's dripping off me, and I wipe my hand over my forehead and neck. Dave leans forward and gently blows on my face. That's the fucking sweetest thing anyone's ever done for me, yeah? I smile and raise my arms above my head for him to blow on my armpits. He buries his face in one instead and I close my arm around his neck and hold him tight. Steve and Josh point and laugh, but fuck it. It feels good. It feels right.

"We fucking off then or what?" Steve asks, spoiling the moment. "You can do your kissy kissy shit when we get home. I've got some DVDs to watch."

Dave pulls away and I reluctantly let him go. "Yeah, I

just need to do something first. Ten minutes, yeah? Here's the keys, I'll meet you back at the car." He tosses a bunch of keys to Josh, who catches it one-handed.

"Ten minutes, eh? Last of the great fucking lovers," Josh says, winking at me.

I watch them walk out through the barn door and reach out for Dave, but he sidesteps me and heads toward the tables in the corner. I follow him and he buys two cans of lager, passes one to me. The can feels hot in my hand, so fuck knows what the lager will taste like. I crack it open and take a long drink, replacing some of the fluids I've lost. It tastes even worse than I expected it to, but fuck it. It's better than nothing.

Dave moves over to the other table, and looks at some DVDs in plastic wallets. They each have two names and a date written on the labels in black marker pen. He buys one that says Buxom Bitch and Scunny Skank with last month's date on it, it costs him a tenner. I look at the others, there's a couple of names I recognise from tonight's fights, but mostly I've never heard of any of them. Dave cradles his DVD to his chest as if it's something precious.

Outside it's fucking freezing and I can't stop shivering. Dave puts his arm around me and leads me toward the farm house. The two gorillas with the baseball bats, Johnno and Baz, stand sentry either side of the front door, glaring at us as we approach.

"What do you want, Davie-boy?" one asks, tapping the bat in the palm of his hand. The other stares at us, unblinking.

"Got someone for Lonnie to see," Dave says.

"Oh yeah? Fresh meat, is she?"

"Yeah."

"Wait there, I'll see if he's got time to see her."

He slips inside, and the other gorilla positions himself in front of the door just in case we had any plans to follow.

"Fresh fucking meat?" I say to Dave.

He grins. "Yeah, that's what they call the fighters. Nothing personal."

"Yeah well it better fucking not be or I'll deck the bastard."

The gorilla comes back and beckons us inside the house. "Lonnie says he'll give you three minutes."

He leads us through the hallway into a large room with lots of computer monitors. Five of them show different views of the cage, and I can see someone mopping the floorboards in there. Other monitors show the interior of the now deserted barn from different angles, the field where the cars used to be, and the outside of the house from every viewpoint you could think of. I can see the front door in one of them, with either Baz or Johnno, whichever one it is, standing outside. I wonder where the camera is hidden, I didn't notice any when we were walking toward the house.

"All right, Lonnie," Dave says.

Lonnie turns out to be a fat bald bloke in his mid-thirties. He sits behind a large oak desk that's covered in piles and piles of money. There must be fucking thousands and thousands on that desk, lying there in neatly stacked rows. Behind him, lounging on a plush leopard-skin settee, is a young man with the smoothest complexion I ever saw. Not a fucking blemish, yeah? He looks like he's just stepped out of an airbrushed magazine photo or something. He's wearing a tight-fitting T-shirt and lycra shorts that show off his physique to perfection. He looks at me with a bored, laid-back expression, then frowns and crosses his legs when he catches me checking out his crotch bulge.

"Who's this you've brought for me then, Davie-boy?" Lonnie says. His voice is soft, much softer than I expected it to be, and slightly nasal. In fact nothing about this

Lonnie geezer is anything like what I expected the boss of an underground fight club to be. I thought he'd be some sort of gangland thug, all knife scars and an evil stare, maybe even a fucking cat to stroke and a moustache to twirl. He looks more like someone you'd see in your granny's slippers and cardigans catalogue. As for his mate on the couch behind him, well fuck knows where you'd see someone like that outside of a porn movie.

"This is Abby," Dave says, gesturing at me.

Lonnie looks me up and down and shrugs. "She any good?" Dave nods. "And you can vouch for her?"

"Yeah, she's sound." Dave glances in my direction and winks.

"Tell you what I'll do," Lonnie says. He folds his arms and leans forward on the desk. "I'll give her a try out in two weeks, just to see how she does. Can't say fairer than that."

"Cheers Lonnie," Dave says. "She won't let you down."

Lonnie smiles. "Oh, I don't doubt it, Davie-boy."

"When do I get paid?" I ask.

Lonnie glances at me, but directs his reply to Dave. "Let's see how she performs first, dear. Tell her to leave her number with Johnno on the way out."

7

Dad's still asleep when I get up for work, but I'm in a good mood so I don't have the TV on too loud while I have my breakfast. I eat my yoghurt thinking about how gentle Dave was, that first time when he took me back to his bedsit after the meeting with Lonnie. I'd been expecting to get jack-hammered, so it was a bit of a surprise. He had a poster of these bald guys on the wall sneering down at me with their fists raised, and when I asked who they were he said they were the best fucking band ever and put on one of their CDs for me to listen to. The bald guys shouted violent songs at us while Dave licked all the stale sweat off every inch of my body. Even when we got down to fucking he kept all his weight off me and took it really slow. Pretty fucking weird it was, but in a nice way.

When I left the next day I thought that'd be the end of it, he got what he wanted so I'd never hear from him again. That's what usually happens anyway. But fuck me if he didn't phone up last night asking if I wanted to go to Shefferham to see some band that's playing there on Saturday. It sounded like a laugh, so I said yeah. It was only after I put the phone down that I remembered I'd promised Shaz I would go to The Zone with her this week. Oh well, fuck it. She could always come along with us, I could fix her up with one of Dave's mates. We're going on our regular Friday night pub crawl tonight, so I'll ask her then.

I make some cheese sandwiches for dad and wrap them up in cling film, put them on the arm of his chair so he'll see them when he gets up, then get the bus into town.

* * *

Blunt the Cunt looks at his watch when I get to work but doesn't say anything. I'm only a couple of minutes late, and it doesn't look like they've started the weekly team-building meeting yet anyway. That's some new bollocks they've come up with at head office. Apparently it's supposed to make us feel like we're part of one big happy family instead of just minimum wage burger monkeys who can either do as we're told or fuck off onto the dole like everyone else our age. Yeah, right.

So every Friday morning we have to fill in a stupid questionnaire about what new skills we've learnt and what we've done to help a fellow team member fulfil their objectives in the last seven days. Then there's a blank page for us to write down our suggestions on how we can improve our customers' happiness index, whatever the fuck that means. There's a weekly prize of five pounds for the best idea, and a hundred pounds if the idea actually gets used nationwide, but nobody from my branch has ever won anything. This week I write "Free blow-job with every burger" and hope for the best. If the idea does get taken up nationally we can always get Colin to do it.

Blunt scoops up the completed forms and reads through them to make sure nobody's said anything bad about him, and sends us off to our designated work areas. Colin heats up last night's leftover burgers and onions on the griddle, Sally spreads the grease around the tables with a dirty cloth, and I take up my usual position by the till. Blunt fucks off into his office to play solitaire or whatever it is he does in there all day.

"Dave phoned last night," I tell Sally. "He's taking me to see some band in Shefferham tomorrow."

"Oh yeah?" Sally looks up from her work, but carries on wiping the tables in a half-hearted way.

"Yeah. He took me to a fight last weekend, it were fucking brilliant."

"Is Dave that skinhead you were going on about last week?"

"Yeah."

Sally scowls. "Rather you than me. I've heard about skinheads from my dad."

"Nah, he might look a bit rough but he's sweet as fuck."

Sally smiles. "Proper fucking gentleman, eh?"

I smile back, remembering what happened when we got back to his bedsit. "Yeah. Yeah, he was."

"So when you gonna bring him here and introduce him to me then?"

"What, so you can throw your knickers at him?"

"Fuck off," she says, grinning, and throws a dirty cloth at me. I duck down and it sails over my head, lands with a squelch on the floor behind me.

The door opens, and the first fat cunt of the day waddles through. This time I don't need to paint the smile on my face, it's already there and it's fucking genuine for a change.

* * *

It's dinner time when my phone rings, the busiest time of day at the burger joint, and the place is full of hungry fat bastards all demanding to be fed. The one at the front of the queue scowls at me when I take out my phone and look at the screen to see who it is. It's Shaz, and I swipe my finger across the screen to answer it.

"Hi Shaz, what's up?"

"Abby, it's Shaz. Just checking you're still on for The Meat Market this week and you haven't found something better to do instead, like you did last week."

Oh fuck. She's not going to like what I've got to tell her.

"Cheeseburger and large fries," the man at the counter says, and I yell the order through to Colin.

"Shaz, I can't make it this Saturday. I'm going to see a

band in Shefferham with Dave and his mates, but you can tag along to that if you want?"

"And how are we supposed to make any money doing that?"

"Well... we won't, it's just a night out isn't it? You know, fun and stuff, yeah?"

I can hear Shaz sigh, a distorted crackle like when someone blows onto a microphone.

"Look, Abby, I don't think you're taking this job seriously enough. I can't afford to lose two weeks' pay, even if you can."

Job? Since when was it a fucking job? It's just a bit of a laugh, not a job. Sure, the money is a nice bonus when we get some, but it's not as if that's the whole point of doing it. Most of the time we're lucky if we make enough to pay for another night out on the piss.

"It's all right for you," Shaz continues, as if she can read my mind, "you've got a proper job. But what about me? I need that money, I can't live without it."

Colin dumps the cheeseburger and fries down on the hatch and I take them to the lard-arse standing by the counter.

"Sorry Shaz, but I already told Dave I'd go."

I hold my hand out for the money, the fat man fumbles in his pocket for his wallet.

"Yeah well," Shaz says. "You need to get your fucking priorities right. I'm not happy about being blown out again just because you've got yourself some fucking cock to rub up against. Sort yourself out, Abby. Otherwise when he fucks off, which we both know he will sooner or later, I won't be here any more."

I ring the order up in the till and hand the fatty his change. He munches into his burger and tomato sauce drips down his shirt. I tell him to have a nice day.

"But we're still on for the piss up tonight, yeah?" I say into the phone.

There's that sigh again. "I suppose," and the line goes dead. Call terminated, the screen says when I look at it.

I put my phone away and look at the next customer. "Yes sir, how may I serve you this fine day?"

* * *

After my workout in the gym I walk home. There's no sign of my dad, and the sandwiches I made for him are still sitting there untouched on the arm of his chair. What the fuck is this, Invasion of the fucking Body Snatchers or something?

"Dad?" I yell. "Are you in?"

No answer. Fuck it, I doubt he'll have gone far.

I make myself something to eat and go upstairs. I tip half a bottle of Matey into the grimy bath and turn the taps on, then head toward my bedroom to find something to wear for the piss-up with Shaz tonight. I'm walking across the landing when I hear a croaky voice coming from my dad's bedroom.

"Is that you Abigail?"

I pop my head round his door and see him lying in bed with the covers pulled up under his chin. His eyes are all red and puffy, I wish he'd remember to take his fucking antihistamines. Maybe if he didn't suffer so much with his allergies he wouldn't be in such a fucking bad mood all the time.

"Are you okay, dad?"

"No."

"Why, what's wrong with you?" I ask.

"Don't know. Everything."

He rolls over to face the wall, and curls himself up into a ball. I can see him shaking under the covers, maybe he's got the flu or something. I ask if he needs anything, but he doesn't reply so I close the door and leave him to it.

8

It takes a few Pernods before Shaz gets out of her massive fucking sulk with me and starts to mellow out. We're in the Black Swan, and being a Friday night it's pretty busy in here. I down my fifth Guinness of the night and elbow my way through the crush around the bar. Fuck knows why people have to stand there drinking all night, they should move out of the way when they've been served. It's just fucking ignorant if you ask me.

"Watch out," someone yells when he doesn't get out of my way quick enough and spills some of his beer down his shirt. I turn and glare at him, he soon gets the message and looks away.

I get myself two pints of Guinness, and three Pernods for Shaz. That should keep us going until closing time, and it'll save me having to go back to the bar later. I pour all the Pernods into one glass, then take a swig out of both pints of Guinness so I can stick my thumb and forefinger into the glasses to make them easier to carry. I make my way back to our table near the jukebox.

There's a guy leaning against the jukebox talking to Shaz. Him and his mate have been eyeing us up since we got here, so it's a surprise he's taken so long to make his move. If it were me I would've told him to fuck off, the last thing I want on a girl's night out is some bloke drooling over me, but Shaz doesn't seem to mind the attention. I slam the drinks down on the table and sit down.

"Hi," the bloke says, grinning at me.

I shrug and reach for my Guinness. "All right," I say.

"Me and Tony over there, we were wondering if we could join you?"

"Yeah, sure," Shaz says. I give her a quick look, she smiles and winks at me.

The bloke beckons this Tony over and he sits down

opposite me, grinning like he's just won the fucking Lottery or something. The other one sits next to Shaz and says his name is Greg. Shaz fingers his forearm and smiles at him. I sip my Guinness while Tony prattles on about football. My eyes glaze over. No wonder he's fucking single, yeah? He stops talking and looks at me. He's probably expecting some sort of answer, but I stopped listening ages ago.

"Dunno," I say with a shrug. Don't fucking care either, whatever it was.

"Really? What about Wazzell then, you think he'll recover in time for the qualifier?"

I shake my head and drain one of my pints of Guinness. "I'm off to the bog, you coming Shaz?"

Shaz nods and struggles to her feet with the help of the table. Squeezing past Greg she stumbles and falls into his lap. He grabs hold of her to stop her from falling to the floor and she puts her arms around his neck to steady herself. She says something to him that makes his face go red, then uses his shoulders to push herself back onto her feet and follows me to the toilet.

"What the fuck did you invite those two losers over for?" I ask once we're inside.

Shaz stands by the mirror, fussing with her hair and pouting at her reflection like one of those fucking movie stars in front of a press photographer. "Thought they might have been a laugh. Anyway, it's not their personality I'm after."

"I'm not screwing around any more, I've got Dave now."

"Dave, Dave, Dave," Shaz says with a sneer. "That's all I hear from you these days. Oh, isn't Dave simply wonderful? Isn't Dave the best thing that's ever happened to me? It's fucking boring."

"Fuck off, I don't say things like that."

"Yeah well, give it time and you soon will be. Anyway, I've got other plans for those two."

Ah, I get it. It's not the contents of their trousers she's after, it's the contents of their wallets. I should have guessed. I go into one of the cubicles for a piss, leaving the door open so I can talk to Shaz at the same time.

"I doubt they've got much on them worth having," I say.

"Yeah well, we can always take them to a cash-point."

"What, and then they just hand over all their money? Doesn't seem very likely."

I finish my piss and wipe myself down with a wad of toilet paper wrapped around my fingers.

"Trust me," Shaz says. "Once they hear about the party we're going to they'll be begging to hand it over."

"What party?" I ask, pulling up my knickers.

Shaz laughs. "There isn't one, but *they* don't need to know that do they?"

"So what's the plan?"

"Just follow my lead," she says, and heads for the door.

I wash my hands and follow her out. By the time I get back to our table Shaz is necking with that Greg bloke. The other one looks at me like he's expecting the same, but fuck that.

"Listen," I say, "um..." It takes me a while to remember his name. "... Tony, me and Shaz are going to a party later if you fancy it?"

Tony's eyes light up and he grins at me. "Sure, that sounds great."

I down my last pint of Guinness in three gulps, and belch in his face. "Well come on then," I say, grinning at his shocked expression. "Oi Shaz, are we off to this fucking party then or what? You can stick your tongue down his throat when we get there."

* * *

Outside, Shaz and Greg sway down the road, arms around each other's waists. Tony puts his arm around my shoulder but it seems forced, like he's a bit embarrassed and not sure what to do.

"Where's the party?" he says.

"Dunno, it's a mate of Shaz. Oi Shaz, where's the party at?"

"Just down here," Shaz says, leading us toward the bank on the main road. "Hey, you know what would be really fucking cool? If we all scored some fucking coke first. What do you reckon Abby?"

I play along, knowing where this is headed. "Yeah, sounds great."

Tony grins at the idea, but Greg doesn't look too happy. "I don't think that's a good idea, what if the police caught us with drugs? I'd lose my job and everything," he whines.

Shaz turns to Greg and gives his crotch a gentle squeeze. "You ever fucked someone when you're coked up? It's the best ever."

You know what they say about men always thinking with their dicks? I reckon it must be fucking true because Greg soon changes his mind.

"How much money have you guys got?" Shaz asks. "I know where I can score some coke, but we'll need to pool our money to get enough to last us the whole night."

"Um, not much," Tony says. "How much would you need?"

"Couple hundred should do it."

"I don't have anywhere near that much," Tony says. He turns to Greg. "How much have you got?"

"Um, about thirty quid?"

"That's not enough," Shaz says. "That's a shame. I was looking forward to a good shag tonight. Oh well, might as well call it a night then. No point going to the party without any coke."

"No, wait," Greg says. "I could get some money from that cash machine over there, I got paid today."

Shaz smiles and gives him a hug. "Well let's go then, lover." She takes him by the hand and leads him to the cash machine.

His hands shake when he puts his card in the machine and types in the pin number. Probably because Shaz is rubbing her hand up and down his crotch while he does it, just in case he might change his mind. When the screen asks how much he wants to withdraw Shaz leans in and prods the £200 selection. Greg's eyes widen, but he doesn't say anything when Shaz taps the 'yes' to confirm the amount. The machine spits out a wad of money and Shaz grabs it, folds it in half and stuffs it into her pocket. She winks at me.

"Well come on then, what are we waiting for?" she says. "Let's get fucking coked up and get down to that party."

Now that's not what I was expecting. I thought once we got the cash we'd just fucking leg it and leave the guys to work it out for themselves. But Shaz must have something else in mind because she drags Greg by the hand toward a back alley. I hope she's not expecting me to shag that fucking Tony loser. Even if I didn't have Dave there's no way I'd want that boring prick bouncing on me.

Then I figure it out. It's to get away from all the fucking cameras on the main road, yeah?

Tony hesitates at the entrance to the alley. He peers into the gloom, watching Shaz and Greg lead the way. He licks his lips, looks around nervously. I take him by the hand, it's cold and clammy. I smile and lean in to whisper in his ear.

"I can't wait to see your cock."

That's all the encouragement he needs to follow me into the alley. Men are so fucking easy to manipulate.

"My dealer's just down here," Shaz says. She turns to

see how far into the alley me and Tony are, and stops to wait for us to catch up. "Just round this next corner, it's not far now."

We turn the corner and Shaz gently pushes Greg against the wall. "You know what would be really great?" she asks.

Greg grins at her and loops his arms around her waist, pulls her closer. "What?"

Shaz smiles back. "This."

She brings her knee up into his bollocks, real quick. His eyes bulge and his face goes purple. He bends over and clutches his hands to his groin, makes this pathetic mewling sound. She kicks him in the knee and it buckles beneath him, sends him sprawling to the ground. She kicks him in the stomach, and most of the beer he's drunk tonight flies out of his mouth.

Tony jumps like a startled flea and tries to pull away from me. I grip his hand tight, holding him in place, and turn toward him. There's a look of sheer fucking terror on his face, and I can't help feeling a bit sorry for him. Wrong place, wrong time, yeah? But I can't lose face in front of Shaz, she already thinks I'm going fucking soft with Dave. I'll just give him a slap and leave it at that. I spin him around and push him face first into the wall, wrench his arm up behind his back. I can feel his body trembling when I lean into him.

"You say anything about this and I'll fucking kill you," I say into his ear. His only answer is a whimper, so I twist the arm a bit higher up his back. "You got that?"

"Yes, yes," he screams, way too fucking loud. Like he's hoping whoever lives in the house at the other side of the wall will hear him and come to his rescue. Well that's when I lose sympathy with him, yeah? I grab a handful of hair and yank his head away from the wall, then slam it back to shut him up. There's a loud crack, and his body goes limp. I let him fall, but don't bother sticking the boot in. I don't bother with his wallet either, somehow it just doesn't feel right. He's just a working class bloke, probably as skint as me.

When I turn around Shaz is still kicking away at Greg, but I doubt he's feeling anything because it looks like he's unconscious too. There's blood pooling around his head, fuck knows where it's coming from but there's a lot of it. Shaz always gets a bit carried away when she's pissed up. One day she'll end up fucking killing someone if she's not careful.

"Shaz, that's enough, yeah?"

Shaz can't resist sticking the boot in one more time before she turns and grins at me. "Yeah, time to get fucked off." She points at Tony. "Did you get the cunt's wallet?"

I look away when I feel my face flush red. "Yeah, but it was empty."

9

Saturday night and I'm standing in a tiny pub on the outskirts of Shefferham with a pint of Guinness in my hand, being jostled by a crowd of skinheads jumping around in front of me while these old geezers on the stage thrash the fuck out of their musical instruments.

I'm wearing an old pair of jeans of mine, and a brown check shirt Dave lent me that's a couple of sizes too big. I blend in quite well with the other women here. Except for my hair, anyway. That's a lot longer than the buzz-cuts they all have.

Shaz stands beside me with her hands over her ears, I don't think she likes this type of music very much. She's dolled up to the fucking nines and sticks out like a randy priest's cock when an altar boy kneels before him. Her tits are threatening to fall out of a low-cut frilly top at any second, and she's wearing a short yellow summer skirt. Fuck knows what sort of band she thought she was going to see, but she'd be more at home at a fucking boy-band concert than here. Mind you, she is getting plenty of admiring leers from all the skinheads, so maybe that's the effect she was after all along.

Dave is somewhere near the front of the stage with Steve and Josh, right in the centre of the melee of flailing arms and legs. He tried to drag me there with him when the band first got on stage, but I don't really want to get any closer to those massive fuck-off speakers than I am now. Even from here the music is so loud it makes my fucking head vibrate.

I never knew there were so many skinheads living around here until we pulled up in Dave's car and saw them all milling around outside the pub. There must be some sort of revival thing going on, because until I met Dave and his mates the other week I don't remember ever seeing any skinheads before. They're all mostly my age too, so they must've picked it up from their parents or something because they wouldn't have even been born the last time skinheads were popular. There's a few old fuckers here as well, including the landlord from The Black Bull and a few of his regulars, but they're all standing at the back, well away from the bustle of the crowd. One of them has a camcorder held above his head, filming the band as they play.

Someone from the crowd climbs on the stage and dives off headfirst into the audience. There's a sudden surge backwards when everyone tries to avoid getting smacked in the face by his flailing hands, and my drink gets knocked by the person in front of me, spilling some of my precious Guinness down the back of his T-shirt. I yell at him and push him in the back and he stumbles forward, loses his balance and falls to his knees. Someone nearby helps him back up onto his feet and he charges into the crowd, grabs hold of a couple of other guys' shoulders and leaps around with them as if nothing's happened.

"This is the last one, you cunts," the singer shouts, "so make the fucking most of it, right? Let's fucking have it, come on, let's go!"

"Thank fuck for that, they're fucking horrible," Shaz shouts in my ear, but before I can reply the music starts up again and everyone goes fucking mental. Even a couple of the oldies from The Black Bull rush into the heart of the crowd and throw themselves around.

I must admit, this type of music is starting to grow on me, so when Shaz tries to pull me toward the toilets I resist. After a few more tugs on my arm and shouted commands that I can't hear she gives up and waits with me until the band finishes their set.

The crowd shout and scream for more, but there's already someone unplugging everything so it looks like that's it for the night. I drink the rest of my Guinness and head toward the bar with Shaz before the inevitable rush when everyone else has the same idea.

I feel a sweaty arm slide around my neck from behind and I spin around with my fist raised, but it's just Dave with his soppy grin. He's got his shirt off, it's tucked into the back of his jeans, and his face and chest are glistening with sweat. I breathe in his aroma and give him a quick kiss but he'll need to dry himself off before he gets anything else.

Dave offers to pay for our drinks and orders a pint each for him and his two mates, and we look around for a table to sit at. The old guy with the camcorder is sitting at the next table, watching his footage on the camera's built-in screen while his mates crowd around him, peering over his shoulder.

"Fucking smart or what?" Dave says.

My ears are ringing so loud I can hardly hear him. I stick my fingers in my ears and wiggle them about, try to clear the high-pitched whistling sound, but it doesn't seem to make any difference.

"Yeah, they were really good," Shaz says, grinning at Josh. He grins back and she slides her chair closer to him. Steve doesn't look too happy about that, I think he's had his eye on Shaz ever since she first got into Dave's car with me.

Dave leans across the table and stares into my eyes. "What did you think of them, Abby?"

I nod. "Yeah, they were okay. A bit old though?"

"That's cos they were original skins, weren't they? They haven't always been old."

"I guess."

"I've got mp3s of all their records at home, I'll play them for you later if you like. Some of their later ones were a bit shite, they went all fucking heavy metal for some reason, but the early ones are fucking classics."

"Are we having a party then?" Shaz asks, looking at Dave.

Dave smiles at her and shakes his head. "Me and Abby are, you and Josh will have to have yours somewhere else."

"Fucking spoilsport," she pouts, and sticks her tongue out. Dave laughs.

"You can come back to mine if you want," Josh says. "But we'll have to be quiet, my dad'll kick you out if we wake him up."

"Not if we give him a good show," Shaz says with a wink.

"I've got my own place," Steve chips in. "Won't matter how much noise we make."

Shaz looks him up and down and smiles. "Well why don't the three of us go there then?"

* * *

We stay until closing time. It's not like we've got a bus to catch or anything, like a lot of the others who had to fuck off at half-ten and leg it down to the bus station. Dave's pretty pissed up, he's swaying a bit when he stands up to go to the toilet, so it's just as well he doesn't need to drive very far. Shaz has got her arms around both the skinheads, one either side of her. All three are laughing and seem to be having a good time, so it seems a shame to break them up. But I need a piss, and there's something I need to check with Shaz before Dave drops them all off on his way home.

"Shaz, are you coming to the bogs with me?"

"Nah, I'm okay," Shaz says, shaking her head.

I stand up and lean across the table. "It's important."

She sighs, and looks up at me. Her shoulders shrug. "Okay boys, I'll see you in a bit." She disentangles herself from the two skinheads and stands up on wobbly feet. She leans on the table for support. Josh puts his hand up her skirt and feels her arse.

"Christ, she's got no fucking knickers on," he yells, overly loud.

Shaz turns and smiles at him, leans down for a kiss. Josh's hand goes back up her skirt.

"In your own fucking time," I say to Shaz.

"Yeah yeah, hold your fucking horses," Shaz says. "We're only having a fucking laugh." Josh looks disappointed when she pulls away and squeezes past him.

"So what's so important then?" Shaz asks when we're in the ladies.

"What are you going to do to Steve and Josh?"

She laughs. "Well what do you think I'm going to do to them? Or rather, what do you think they're going to do to me?"

"I mean after that. What are you going to do to them after you've had your fun?"

She shrugs. "Depends how good they are."

"Look, Shaz, I like Dave. A lot. I don't want you to hurt his mates."

"Girl, you're going fucking soft. Men are just walking cocks with wallets. Think of them as anything else and they'll trample all over you. Is that what you want?"

"Dave's not like that," I say. Perhaps a little bit too quickly because Shaz laughs in my face. "Just don't hurt them, yeah?"

"Relax, I wasn't going to."

"And don't take their money either."

She frowns. "Aw, you're no fun anymore, you know that Abby?"

"Promise me, yeah?"

Shaz smiles and holds up two fingers. "Dib fucking dib. Dob fucking dob. Satisfied?"

I nod because that's probably the best I'm likely to get from her. But if she does hurt them in any way I'll never forgive her.

Outside in the car park there's a police snatch-wagon with two ugly fuckers standing beside it in full riot gear. They glare at us through their visors as we leave the pub. Fucking bastards, haven't they got anything better to do, like look for my mum? Dave spits on the ground when he sees them, I guess he doesn't like the cunts much either. They watch us walk up to Dave's car.

It takes Dave a while to fit his key into the lock, in the end he has to put a hand over one eye before he can hit the right spot. There's a thunk and the door unlocks. Dave opens it, reaches in, and unlocks the other doors. Shaz gets in the back, sandwiched between the two skinheads. I walk around the front of the car, keeping a wary eye on the two police thugs, and get in the passenger side.

Dave manages to fit the keys into the ignition and the engine roars into life. He fumbles with the CD player while he revs the engine, and loud music blares out. I lean my elbow over the open window and tap on the side of the car with my fingers in time to the music. Yeah, it's definitely starting to grow on me.

Dave leans forward and peers through the windscreen like an old man who's lost his spectacles. The coppers are still watching us, but if they were going to say anything they would've done it by now. Dave puts the car in gear and we roll forward through the car park. We bounce over the kerb, onto the main road, and pull away. He drives very slowly, with one hand on the steering wheel, the other firmly clamped over his left eye. Even when we reach the winding country road that leads to our town he doesn't go much above fifty, and slows right down for the bends instead of screeching through them like he did on the journey to Shefferham earlier tonight. And they say alcohol makes people bad drivers, yeah? If anything the booze has improved Dave's driving skills no fucking end.

We pull up outside a dilapidated-looking terrace house with six doorbells on the front door, and the two skinheads climb out of either side of the car. Shaz leans forward between the front seats and breathes Pernod fumes at me.

"See you Shaz. I'll give you a ring tomorrow, yeah?"

I lean forward and shuffle myself around in my seat to face her. "Don't forget what I said."

She holds up two fingers and grins. "I won't." She leans back and shuffles herself out of the car. Her skirt rides up her legs, showing everything she's got like a third-rate celebrity hoping to make the newspaper front pages. Josh reaches out to help her onto her feet while Steve takes out a key and opens the front door of the house.

"See you Dave, have fun," Steve says, leaning into the car.

Dave grins and nods his farewell. "You too, mate." He turns to me when Josh slams the car door behind him. "Right then, let's get fucked off shall we?"

10

Dad's in a massive fucking sulk when I go back home on Sunday night. It's like he doesn't want me to have a life of my own or something and he's determined to make me suffer for every second of fun I might have. He's sat in his chair in his pyjamas, watching TV when I get there. Probably been sitting there all fucking weekend, knowing him.

"Huh. You're back then are you?" he says when I slump down on the settee. "I don't know why you bother coming home, you might as well just leave like your mum did."

Yeah well, I don't know why I bother either, it's not like I get any appreciation for everything I do for him. If it wasn't for work tomorrow I would've stayed at Dave's bedsit, fucking and listening to his skinhead music all day. But I'm not going to give dad the argument he obviously wants. It's been a fucking brilliant weekend, and I don't want anything to pull me down from the emotional high I'm on.

"I'm going to bed if you're going to be like that," I tell him. "I'll see you tomorrow."

Dad scowls. "Yeah, that's right. You go to bed and leave me on my own again. Like you've left me on my own all weekend, and you'll be leaving me on my own again tomorrow. I don't care any more, so just do what you want."

Fine, I think, I'll fucking do that then, you miserable old bastard, but I resist the urge to say it out loud. I'm not interested in playing his fucking mind games tonight.

* * *

Next morning I get up and make dad some sandwiches for while I'm at work. He's still asleep, fuck knows what

85

time he went to bed last night but I didn't hear him clumping around like I usually do. I half expected him to be still sat there watching TV when I came downstairs, ready to start up his whinge-fest from where he left off last night.

I switch on the TV and tune into one of the music channels. It all seems really slow and boring after listening to Dave's music all weekend, but it will have to do. I turn up the volume so I can hear it from the kitchen.

There's not much in the fridge, so it looks like dad will have to settle for cheese sandwiches again today. I'll do a shop after work, maybe I can sneak off early and get Sally to cover for me.

I've been watching some of Dave's DVDs of the female fights on his computer, studying their moves and planning out what I would've done if I was on the receiving end of them. Dave watched them with me but they made him randy after a while, so I had to fight him off and ended up missing a few bits. Still, I think I've got them all sussed out now. I don't know which one I'll be fighting, Dave says the bouts aren't finalised until the day before and I won't find out who it is until I get there on the night.

I'm just about to put dad's cheese sandwiches on the arm of his chair when I hear him thumping down the stairs.

"You're still here then?" he says, stating the fucking obvious. I can tell by the look on his face he's still in a mood about me staying the weekend with Dave.

"I made you some breakfast," I say. I smile and point at the sandwiches.

Dad storms across the room and swipes the plate onto the floor. "I don't want any breakfast!" he yells.

"Fine," I say. "Do without then."

I kick off my slippers and get my boots from the hallway. I sit down on the settee and lace them up.

"And where do you think you're going?" dad says,

glaring at me from his armchair.

"I'm going to work."

"What about this mess you've made?"

I look at him, speechless, and shake my head. I stand up and head for the door. Fuck this, there's no reasoning with him when he's like this. I slam the door behind me.

* * *

"Can you step into my office please, Abby?" Cunty Blunty says as soon as I walk through the door.

Sally gives me a quick look, then turns away. She doesn't smile like she usually does when I arrive at work. Something's up, I can feel it. Fucking great, what have I done now? It's not like I'm late again, there's still a few more minutes before my shift is due to start.

I sigh, and walk toward the office at the back of the burger joint. Blunt's standing there holding the door open for me. I give him a quizzical look and he gestures for me to enter. Inside there's some fat bastard in a flash suit, probably an area manager or something. He stands up and looks at me.

"Hello Abby, remember me?"

I look at him and shrug. "Should I?"

He smiles, but there's no warmth behind it. "Oh yes, I should say so."

Blunt sits behind his desk and steeples his fingers on its surface. He stares at me and frowns. "Mr Green has made a serious allegation against you Abby, what do you have to say about it?"

"Well it would help if I knew what it was?"

"Oh come on," the fat man says, "as if you don't know."

I look at him. He's got one of those faces that you just want to punch, yeah? All smug and smarmy, like he owns the fucking world or something. He does look vaguely familiar, but fuck knows who he is.

"Mr Green says you stole some money from him," Blunt says.

"As if," I say, folding my arms.

"Oh yes you did," the fat man says. "Outside The Zone two weeks ago, you and another girl."

I sneer at him. So that's where I've seen him before. "Oh yeah, you're that fucking pervert who pays to have sex with young girls."

His face goes red, looks like it's about to explode. "You know full well that's not what happened. You stole my money."

"Did I fuck. You gave us your money so we wouldn't report you to the police, you fucking nonce."

"Now look here–"

"Okay Mr Green, I can handle it from here," Blunt says. "So you admit you have this man's money?"

I shrug.

"Of course she does," the fatty says. "Now what are you going to do about it?"

Blunt stares at me and I stare back. He shakes his head and sighs, then leans back in his chair and looks at the fat cunt. "From what you've told me I think this is more a matter for the police."

"No, there's no need for that," he says quickly.

I turn to face him and smile. "Oh, I wonder why not."

"Just give me the money back and we'll say no more about the matter. I can't say fairer than that."

"Fuck off, you fat pervert."

"That's enough, Abby," Blunt says. "Wait outside, I'll deal with you in a minute."

I give fatty one last glare, then pull open the door. Sally nearly falls through it. She darts to one side and I walk out, slam the door behind me.

"Christ Abby," Sally says, "what the fuck have you been

doing now?"

"Nothing, he's full of shit."

We both put our ears to the door, but all I can hear is murmurs. Then the door opens and the fat man walks out, smiling to himself. He brushes past me and I resist the urge to kick him in the arse as he waddles away.

"Come in please Abby," Blunt says from inside the office.

Sally taps me on the back. "Good luck." I smile at her and walk into the office, close the door behind me.

Blunt gestures at a chair. "Sit down, Abby."

"I'll stand, thanks."

If I'm going to get a bollocking I'd rather he had to do it looking up at me. Gives me more power, yeah? He looks up at me, nods his head slowly.

"Look, there's no easy way to put this, so I'll just come straight out with it. We need to make some efficiency savings, so I'm making you redundant. It's nothing personal."

"You what? You mean you're sacking me over what that fucking pervert said?"

"No, no, the two matters are entirely separate. If Mr Green wants to pursue the matter with the police that's his affair. Like I said, we need to make efficiency savings. I've thought long and hard about which one of you I was going to have to let go, it hasn't been an easy decision at all."

"Like fuck it hasn't, you pompous prick. You've always had it in for me."

Blunt frowns and clasps his hands together. "To be perfectly honest, I don't feel you're very well suited to the catering industry. Your attitude toward customers leaves a lot to be desired."

"Fuck you," I yell, and turn to leave. "I'll take you to a fucking tribunal for this, you can't just sack me over what some cunt says I did in my own time."

"Like I said Abby, the two matters are entirely separate. But I take it you don't keep up with the news?" I turn back and he smiles at me in that smug bastard way of his. "By all means take it to a tribunal, but they'll only tell you employers have a lot more flexibility in ridding themselves of unwanted staff these days."

* * *

I'm still fuming when I walk into the goth shop. The lights are dim, the walls and ceiling are painted black, and there's some weird, wailing music playing. It's the first time I've ever been in here, so I don't know which of the five ghouls staring at me work here and which ones are just customers. I glance at the freaky clothes hanging on rails along the wall and wonder what sort of person would want to wear them.

I walk around the shop and find what I'm looking for near the counter, on top of a glass cabinet filled with assorted drugs paraphernalia. Stash tins, packets of massive Rizzlas, big glass bongs with multi-coloured tubes coming out of them, things like that. There's a sign on the cabinet saying *For decorative use only, not to be used for illegal purposes*. Yeah, right.

It's the studded wristbands on top I'm interested in. I spin the rotary display, looking for one that's a decent size. They're mostly just a thin leather strip with one line of conical studs, neither use nor ornament. There's one with spiked studs that catches my eye. The spikes are quite long, and look like they would do some serious damage if you wrapped it around your knuckles. Probably a bit too much damage though, yeah? I don't want to fucking maim anyone.

I pick up a large wristband with seven rows of pyramid

studs and try it on. It's a bit fiddly to get the straps fastened with one hand, but I manage it in the end and flex my arm to try it out for size. The leather's a bit stiff with it being new, and it feels weird, but I'm sure I'll get used to that in time.

I lift up my arm to inspect the price tag dangling from a bit of string tied to the buckle. Fuck me, how much? I was hoping to buy two, but it looks like I'll have to make do with one. I take it to the counter, and a young ghoul blinks at me before taking up a position by the till. His face and hair are pure white, like someone's dipped him head-first in a tin of emulsion paint, and he's wearing black lipstick. I get a sudden urge to punch him in the face, but I somehow manage to resist it.

"You want me to put it in a bag for you?" he says.

"Nah, I'll wear it now."

He picks up a pair of scissors and snips off the price tag, puts it in a black box next to the till. I pay him his extortionate amount of money and leave the shop.

I wonder if dad's still in a mood while I make my way to the supermarket. He probably is, but if I get him some cans of Special Brew I'm sure he'll cheer up after he drinks them. Either that or fall asleep in front of the TV, which is just as good for me. Fuck knows how he'll react when I tell him I lost my job.

I collect a shopping trolley from outside the supermarket and push it through the door toward the drinks aisle. One of the wheels is wonky, it squeaks and pulls the trolley to one side. It takes a while to get the hang of pushing it in a straight line, I need to push it at a slight angle to compensate for the fucked up steering.

I pick up a four-pack of Special Brew and drop them into the trolley. Hopefully that will be enough because I blew most of my spare money on the wristband and I still need to re-stock the fridge.

I reach into a big coffin freezer for a bag of frozen chips. Dad likes the curly ones best, but there's not many left and I need to bend right over to reach one of the few remaining bags at the bottom of the freezer.

"Hello Abigail."

The voice makes me jump, and I nearly lose my balance and topple into the freezer. I push myself upright and spin around, grinning like a little kid.

"Mum!"

She's smiling too, but the man who's with her isn't. I look at him and he looks away quickly and pretends to find something interesting among the tins of soup on the shelf opposite. He's wearing a tweed jacket with leather patches on the elbows, and matching trousers. He looks like someone out of one of those fucking Country Life magazines for posh cunts, someone who likes to shoot small animals for fun, and I take an instant dislike to him.

"How have you been, Abigail?" mum asks.

I frown. "Never mind that, where have you been? And who's that?" I point my thumb at the man's back.

Mum looks embarrassed, and so she fucking well should be. "That's just Cedric from work," she says a little bit too quickly. "I, um, had to get away. You know what it's like living with your dad, I just can't cope with him any more."

"What, and you couldn't tell me you were going? You couldn't phone so we'd know you were okay? Dad's worried sick about you, he thinks you're lying dead somewhere."

"How is your dad?"

"Well how do you think he is? He's not eating, and he spends more time sulking in bed than anything else."

"Has he been taking his medication?"

She must mean his antihistamines. It seems a stupid thing to ask, given the circumstances, but I nod anyway.

"Yeah. I think he might have skipped a few, but I've

been making sure he has one every day."

Mum looks relieved. "Oh, thank god for that."

"So when are you coming back home?"

Mum looks at the man in the tweed jacket before she replies. "I'm not, Abigail. I have a new life now."

"What, with him?"

The man walks over and puts his arm around mum's shoulder. I glare at him. I want to kick his fucking head in. Mum starts to cry, and he strokes her hair.

"It's okay, Barbara," he says, looking at me.

This is too fucking much for me to take. I turn and leave them to it. Leave my shopping trolley behind and head for the door. This is fucked up. Mum's too old to be having affairs, she should be at home looking after dad.

11

"You got nothing, bitch. You're going down and I'm gonna stomp your fucking pretty little head to a pulp," the female gorilla says while we wait for the dolly-bird in the red knickers to finish prancing around in the cage on the other side of the door. Johnno looks at me to see if I'll react to her taunts. I fold my arms and smile at her, Johnno goes back to watching the dolly-bird through a crack in the door.

It's the night of my big fight, and adrenalin surges through me. My opponent's hair is as close-cropped as Dave and his two mates, and she's got more muscle than the three of them combined. There's a deep scar down the left side of her face, and her nose is crooked like it's been broken several times. There's more scars on her arms, criss-crosses of tiny cuts turning her tattoos into mosaics. Scunny Skank is her cage name, and if it wasn't for her tits I'd swear she was a fucking man.

I've seen her in action on one of Dave's DVDs, and I know she's just trying to make me angry so I'll lose control once we're inside the cage. That's one of her tactics, egging her opponent on and then taking advantage of the mistakes they make in anger, but it won't work on me. She's pretty slow, and relies on those massive fists of hers more than anything else. With the size of her there's not a lot else she could do, and that will work in my favour as long as I don't get too close. I'm pretty confident I can take this bitch down.

They called me Stabby Abby. A fucking stupid name if you ask me, but I didn't get any choice in the matter. I guess whichever fucking brainbox comes up with these things couldn't think of anything else. Could be worse, I suppose, thinking about some of the names of the other female fighters on Dave's DVDs.

Scunny Skank bares her yellow teeth at me with a snarl. I guess she's too fucking stupid to think about using a gum shield because she's hardly got any teeth left at the front, just two up and three down. Hopefully I'll get a chance to do a bit of dentistry on her myself in the near future and even them up a bit. Me, I'm not taking any chances like that. I like to chew my food, yeah? I swiped a gum shield from Big Al's gym the other day, and I'm wearing a chest protector under my vest that I got from the sports shop. It's designed for fencing, but it should do just as well with fists.

The cage door opens and the bird in the red knickers flounces out with her placard, shivering from the sudden change in temperature. Johnno steps forward and drapes a fur coat around her shoulders and she draws it around herself. She looks blankly at me and Scunny Skank while we continue staring each other out.

"You go in first," Johnno says to me.

With a final smile at my opponent I turn away. The heat as I walk into the cage is fucking intense, it's like walking into an oven, and the sweat starts to pour after a few seconds. The crowd cheers my entrance, and I raise my left fist to them, showing off my new studded wristband. The cheering gets louder as I strut around the cage, posing for the cameras. I can see Shaz standing near the bars with Dave and his skinhead mates, she's shouting something but I can't hear it over the crowd because they've just gone fucking mental over the entrance of Scunny Skank. She must be their favourite to win or something because her cheer is a lot louder than mine was.

I retire to a corner of the cage while she has her moment in the limelight. She's doing some sort of fucking war-dance or something, legs apart like one of those fat bastard sumo wrestlers on the telly. She's got her back to me, I could easily run up and kick her in the arse before she even knew what was happening, but that wouldn't be sporting would it? Instead I just practice my footwork, jab the air with my fists, and wait for the bell.

And here it is, just seconds after Scunny Skank moves to her corner and turns to face me. Ding fucking dong, round one of one. She runs at me, arms outstretched to grab me in a bear hug. I wait until she's close and then duck under her arms just as she brings her hands together. I keep moving and spin around behind her, ready to smack her on the back of the head with my studded wristband, but she's quicker than I expected at regaining her balance and turns to face me. She shouts something and spits in my face, I throw a punch at her midriff and dance backwards out of reach. I can feel her phlegm dripping down my cheek, it's quite cooling in a way. I wipe it with my hand, smear it around the rest of my face.

She lunges at me again, and this time I let her come. She swings her fist, but there's no real control to it, she just lashes out blindly. I raise my left arm to meet it, and her knuckles graze across the studded wristband. There's a lot of power behind her punch, I can feel it juddering through my arm. I swing with my right fist, catch her on the side of her unprotected chin, and her head turns with the blow. Spit flies from her mouth, showering me again.

I aim for her knee with my boot, kicking out sideways, hoping it will put her down. She must be expecting it because she steps backwards and spins around, her arms outstretched like fucking Jesus doing an impersonation of a spinning top. One of those massive fists glances across the side of my head and I stumble to one side. She grabs me in a bear hug, pins my arms by my sides, and pushes me up against the bars.

I can feel someone outside the cage groping my arse through the bars. The crowd are shouting for blood, and it's mine they want. Scunny Skank screams in my face and stamps down on my foot. Thank fuck for the steel toe-caps, I don't feel a thing. But then she nuts me in the face, and that I *do* feel. A blinding white light between my eyes, and a sharp pain on the bridge of my nose. I kick out at her shins, one after the other. She breaks her hold on me and grabs me by the right wrist, spins me around. I run with the spin, knowing she's going to let go at any moment to send me crashing into the bars. But I'm ready for that.

She lets go and I stumble toward the bars like she expects me to. She's close behind, ready to finish me off, and looks surprised when I crouch down and dodge between her legs. She doesn't even have time to reach down to grab me. She spins around and I grab her by the neck, digging my fingernails in as I squeeze. I raise my left arm and bring the studded wristband down on top of her head. She grins at me and drives a fist into my stomach. The breath is sucked out of me, and I get that *Oh no I'm going to fucking drown* panic you always get when your muscles tense up and refuse to do what they're supposed to do, but I try to ignore it. It'll pass, it always does. Just keep squeezing the bitch's neck and she'll be in the same position as me soon enough.

She makes a grab for my hair and yanks my head to one side. My lungs start to work again, letting me yell out in pain. It's fucking obvious now, but I really should have shaved it off before the fight like Dave had suggested. I told him to fuck off, I like my hair just the way it is. That was a mistake I'm regretting now.

I can't help bending over as she yanks my hair down, and I lose my grip around her neck. She brings her knee up into my face and I fall back onto my arse, dazed. She's on me in an instant, and straddles me with her knees holding my arms by my sides. Her massive fists pummel my already smarting head, one after the other. I can taste copper in my mouth, something warm and wet pouring from my nose. I turn my head to one side as another fist flies toward me, and spray the floorboards with blood. The fist smacks me in the ear, making it burn and whistle.

I squirm my body, try to free my hands so I can get at her. She grins down at me, saliva dripping from her mouth. I manage to twist one hand around and dig my fingernails into her thigh. She flinches, and her weight shifts slightly to one side. I bring my knee up into her cunt. It takes a few tries to hit the right spot, but when I do she squeals like a fucking pig at a slaughterhouse. I knee her again in the same spot and she slumps down on top of me like a dead weight, crushing me.

I wrench my shoulder upwards, twisting my body at the same time. She starts to topple off me and I get my arm free, help her on her way with a shove. She rolls onto her back and clutches her rancid cunt with both hands. Her face screws up in pain. I roll over onto my hands and knees and crawl toward her. I push myself upright onto my knees and clasp my hands together, raise them above my head. I scream as I bring them crashing down into her fucking ugly face and splatter her nose all over it.

I lean on her chest while I struggle to my feet. Her hand darts out and grabs my ankle. I lose my balance and tumble backwards, land hard and crack the back of my head on the floorboards. I roll onto my side, dazed. Scunny Skank crawls toward me on her hands and knees, blood dripping from her face. She grins at me like a fucking demented demon.

"Fucking get up, Abby," I hear someone yelling over the roar of the crowd. I think it might be Shaz, but it could just as easily be me.

My head's spinning like fuck and I can't think straight. All I know is I can't let that fucking bitch get back on top of me again or I'm finished. I roll onto my stomach and crawl to the cage bars. People outside shout and wave their fists at me. I grab the bars, start to pull myself up. My hands slip down, leaving a trail of blood behind them. Where the fuck did that come from?

I struggle to my knees and try to summon up the strength to pull myself onto my feet. Someone yells in my ear, "Fucking die, you bitch!" If I could see straight I would make a note of the bastard's face so I can twat him later, but all I see is a fuzzy haze of blurred faces all yelling and screaming at me.

I look over my shoulder. Scunny Skank is only a few feet away, still crawling toward me. I scream at the crowd in rage, and wrench on the bars. My arms ache, my hands slip, but I slowly pull myself up. I slide my hands further up the bars and get my feet under me, push up with my knees. Just one more push and I'll be there.

I feel fingers clasp around my ankle, and a primal scream behind me that's loud enough to drown out the noise of the crowd. I spin and lash out with my foot, not caring what I hit. It hits her in the temple. Steel toe-caps make a dull thud and send her spinning away from me. I stagger toward her. She rolls over, struggles to sit up. I kick her in the face and send her back down again. She stares up at me, her eyes blazing, her fingers twitching by her sides. I stamp down on her tits and she screams, her hands flail up to protect them. I crouch down by her side and lean over her, my face inches away from hers. My blood drips onto her face.

"Not so fucking tough after all, yeah?"

She stares up at me, like she wants to fucking kill me. I reach down and grab her ears, twist them as I pull her head off the floorboards. I slam her head down as hard as I can. Her eyes roll up, but they're soon back staring at me again. For fuck's sake, what is she some sort of fucking Terminator or what? I struggle back to my feet and kick her in the side of the head. She rolls over, blood spraying. She starts to push herself up with her arms, I kick her in the head again. She goes down. Stays down.

I turn away from her and stagger to the centre of the cage. I raise my arms, fists clenched, and roar. The crowd roars with me, and it's the best fucking feeling ever. They're chanting, "Abby, Abby, Abby, Abby," and I turn around slowly, basking in it. I can see Dave grinning at me, Shaz jumping up and down in excitement by his side. Hands reach through the cage bars, just trying to touch me as I make a triumphant circuit.

Then the cage door opens, the doctor rushes in, and the crowd peels away in search of liquid refreshment. I glance at Shaz and Dave, still standing there by the bars, and stagger through the open door.

12

I'm lying on Dave's bed with my legs in the air while he slides in and out of me. I try to make the right moaning sounds to encourage him, but my head's not really in it. I'm covered in cuts and bruises from the fight, woozy as fuck from all the painkillers I've taken, and I just want him to shoot his load so I can go to fucking sleep. Thank fuck he's keeping all his weight off me, that's all I can say. I'm sure one of my ribs is cracked, I should probably go down to the hospital in the morning and get myself checked out.

The money I got from the fight is spread all over the bed. It seems a bit weird fucking someone when you've got the queen's face stuck to your arse, but I've never had this much money before and the thrill of seeing it covering the entire bed is something that will stay with me forever. I don't know how long it will last now I've joined the ranks of the unemployed, but fuck it. I'm going to enjoy it while I can.

Dave's making his gurning face, and he's going faster now, so it looks like he's nearly finished. I reach around and grab his arse, he spurts into me and I moan up at him and pretend to shudder. He bends down and blows the sweat from my forehead then gets back up on his knees and stretches his arms out. He smiles down at me.

"Why don't you move in?" he says, and wipes his cock on a five pound note. He lies down next to me, waiting for an answer.

I don't know what to say. I mean, it's just come out of the fucking blue, yeah? I can feel his spunk dribbling out of me, I should probably do something about that before it reaches the money, but all I can think of is what he's just asked me. I smile and close my eyes. Moving into Dave's bedsit is a big step, and I don't know if I'm ready for it. He makes me feel good, there's no denying that. It's like I'm walking on air when I'm with him, and I get this fucking weird aching feeling when I'm not. But I know from my own parents that won't last long. The mutual hatred will soon set in, then we'll be yelling and screaming at each other all day.

But then again, maybe we could somehow be the exception to that particular rule?

I open my eyes. Dave's asleep. Oh well, at least that gives me more time to think about it. I roll over onto my side and put my head against his chest, listen to his heartbeat. He murmurs in his sleep and an arm flies around me. I snuggle closer and close my eyes. I like things with Dave just the way they are. That daft grin of his, the gentle way he fucks me, the places he takes me, the way he pays me attention even when he's with his mates, the way he always—

My eyes snap open.

What the fuck? I'm starting to think like a fucking girl. I'll be wanting to get fucking married next, and start producing sprogs with him.

But would that be such a bad idea? Give up the fighting, boozing and partying for good, swap it all for a life of domesticity with Dave?

Nah, fuck that. It must be the fucking painkillers messing with my mind, yeah?

Printed in Great Britain
by Amazon

48581056R10059